'I'm Tracy Beaker. This is a book all about me. I'd read it if I were you. It's the most incredible dynamic heart-rending story. Honest.'

THE STORY OF TRACY BEAKER

Meet Tracy in her first ever story. Tracy is ten years old. She lives in a Children's Home but would like a real home one day, with a real family.

STARRING TRACY BEAKER

Tracy is back – and this time she's determined to be a star! When she's cast in the main role in her school play, her biggest worry is whether her mum will make it back from Hollywood in time to see her perform . . .

THE DARE GAME

The third Tracy Beaker book – join Tracy as she tries out living with Cam, and living on her own in a very unusual place . . .

READ ALL OF TRACY'S ADVENTURES!

www.jacquelinewilson.co.uk

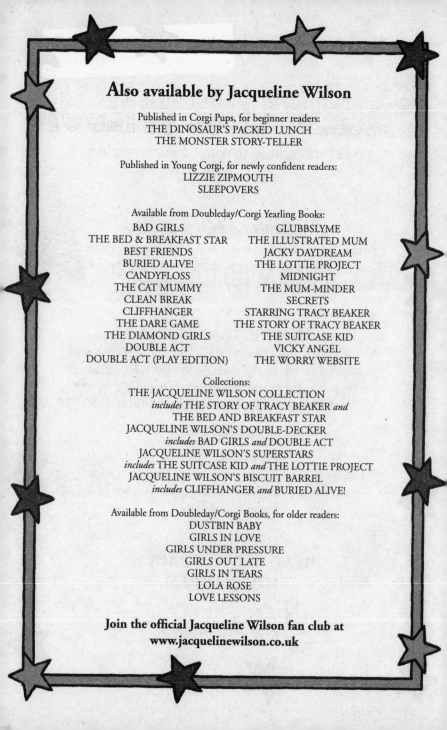

Also available by Jacqueline Wilson

Published in Corgi Pups, for beginner readers:
THE DINOSAUR'S PACKED LUNCH
THE MONSTER STORY-TELLER

Published in Young Corgi, for newly confident readers:
LIZZIE ZIPMOUTH
SLEEPOVERS

Available from Doubleday/Corgi Yearling Books:

BAD GIRLS
THE BED & BREAKFAST STAR
BEST FRIENDS
BURIED ALIVE!
CANDYFLOSS
THE CAT MUMMY
CLEAN BREAK
CLIFFHANGER
THE DARE GAME
THE DIAMOND GIRLS
DOUBLE ACT
DOUBLE ACT (PLAY EDITION)

GLUBBSLYME
THE ILLUSTRATED MUM
JACKY DAYDREAM
THE LOTTIE PROJECT
MIDNIGHT
THE MUM-MINDER
SECRETS
STARRING TRACY BEAKER
THE STORY OF TRACY BEAKER
THE SUITCASE KID
VICKY ANGEL
THE WORRY WEBSITE

Collections:
THE JACQUELINE WILSON COLLECTION
includes THE STORY OF TRACY BEAKER *and*
THE BED AND BREAKFAST STAR
JACQUELINE WILSON'S DOUBLE-DECKER
includes BAD GIRLS *and* DOUBLE ACT
JACQUELINE WILSON'S SUPERSTARS
includes THE SUITCASE KID *and* THE LOTTIE PROJECT
JACQUELINE WILSON'S BISCUIT BARREL
includes CLIFFHANGER *and* BURIED ALIVE!

Available from Doubleday/Corgi Books, for older readers:
DUSTBIN BABY
GIRLS IN LOVE
GIRLS UNDER PRESSURE
GIRLS OUT LATE
GIRLS IN TEARS
LOLA ROSE
LOVE LESSONS

**Join the official Jacqueline Wilson fan club at
www.jacquelinewilson.co.uk**

JACQUELINE WILSON

The Dumping Ground

STARRING
TRACY BEAKER

Illustrated by
Nick Sharratt

CORGI YEARLING

STARRING TRACY BEAKER
A CORGI YEARLING BOOK 978 0 440 86819 4

First published in Great Britain by Doubleday,
an imprint of Random House Children's Books

Doubleday edition published 2006
Corgi Yearling edition published 2007

3 5 7 9 10 8 6 4

RANDOM HOUSE CHILDREN'S BOOKS
61–63 Uxbridge Road, London W5 5SA

www.kidsatrandomhouse.co.uk

Addresses for companies within The Random House Group Limited
can be found at: www.randomhouse.co.uk/offices.htm

THE RANDOM HOUSE GROUP Limited Reg. No. 954009

A CIP catalogue record for this book is available from the British Library.

Printed in the UK by CPI Bookmarque, Croydon, CR0 4TD

*To the staff and pupils at
Charles Dickens Primary School*

I'm Tracy Beaker. Mark the name. I'll be famous one day.

I live in a children's home. We all call it the Dumping Ground. We're dumped here because no one wants us.

No, that's total rubbish. My mum wants me. It's just she's this famous film star and she's way too busy making movies in Hollywood to look after me. But my mum's coming to see me at Christmas. She *is*. I just know she is.

'Your mum's not coming to see you in a month of Sundays,' said Justine Littlewood. 'Your mum's never ever coming back because she doesn't want anything to do with an ugly manky bad-mouthed stupid show-off who wets the bed every ni—'

She never managed to finish her sentence because I leaped across the room, seized hold of her hair and yanked hard, as if I was gardening and her hair was a particularly annoying weed.

I ended up in the Quiet Room. I didn't care. It gave me time to contemplate. That's a posh word for think. I have an extensive vocabulary. I am definitely destined to be a writer. A *successful* glossy rich and famous writer, not a struggling scruffy hack like Cam.

Cam ←

I mused (*another* posh word for think!) over the idea of a month of Sundays.

It would be seriously cool to have a lie-in every single day and watch telly all morning and have a special roast dinner and never have to go to school. But then I pondered (posh alternative number *three*) on the really bad thing about Sundays. Lots of the kids in the Dumping Ground get taken out by their mums or dads.

I don't. Well, I see Cam now, that's all. Cam's maybe going to be my foster mum. She's going to classes to see if she's suitable. It's mad. I don't trust my stupid social worker, Elaine the Pain. I don't want Cam to get cold feet. Though she keeps her toes cosy in her knitted stripy socks. She's not what you'd call a natty dresser. She's OK. But a foster mum isn't like a *real* mum. Especially not a famous glamorous movie star

Elaine the Pain

9

mum like mine. It isn't *her* fault she hasn't shown up recently. She's got such a punishing film schedule that, try as she might, she simply can't manage to jump on a plane and fly over here.

But she *is* going to come for Christmas, so there, Justine Now-Almost-Bald-And-It-Serves-You-Right Littlewood. My mum promised. She really really did.

She was going to see me in the summer. We were going to have this incredible holiday together on a tropical island, lying on golden sands in our bikinis, swimming with dolphins in an azure sea, sipping cocktails in our ten-star hotel . . .

Well, she was going to take me out for the day. It was all arranged. Elaine the Pain set it all up – but my poor mum couldn't make it. Right at the last minute she was needed for some live television interview – I'm sure that was it. Or maybe *Hello!* or *OK!* magazine wanted an exclusive photo shoot. Whatever.

So she never showed up, and instead of being understanding I heard Elaine ranting on to Jenny at the Dumping Ground, telling her all sorts of stupid stuff, like I was crying my eyes out. That was a downright lie. I would never cry. I sometimes get a little attack of hay fever, but I never cry.

I felt *mortified*. I wanted to cement Elaine's mouth shut. We had words. Quite a few of mine were bad words. I told Elaine that she had no business talking about one of her clients – i.e. me – and I had a good mind to report her. It was outrageous of her slandering my mum. She was a famous Hollywood movie actress, didn't she *understand*? Elaine should be more *deferential*, seeing as she's just a poxy social worker.

Elaine said a bad word then. She said she understood why I was so angry. It was easier for me to take my anger out on her when I was *really* angry at my mum for letting me down yet again. *WHAT???* I wasn't the slightest bit angry with my mum. It wasn't her fault she's so popular and famous and in demand.

'Yeah, so why haven't we ever seen her in a single film or telly show, and why are there never any photos of her in any of the magazines?' said Justine Why-Won't-She-Mind-Her-Own-Business Littlewood.

'Wash your ears out, Justine Littlewood. My mum's a famous *Hollywood* actress. Like, Hollywood in America. She isn't in films and mags over *here*, but in America she's incredibly well known. She can't set foot outside the door without the photographers snapping away and all her fans begging for autographs.'

'Yeah, yeah, she signs all these autographs, yet when does she ever bother to write to you?' said Justine Won't-Ever-Quit Littlewood.

But ha ha, sucks to you, J.L., because my mum *did* write, didn't she? She sent me a postcard.

She really did.

I keep it pinned on my wall, beside the photo of Mum and me when I was a baby and still looked sweet. The postcard had a picture of this cutesie-pie teddy with two teardrops falling out of his glass eyes and wetting his fur and the word *Sorry!* in sparkly lettering.

On the back my mum wrote:

So sorry I couldn't make it, Tracy. Chin up, chickie! See you soon. Christmas?
Lots of love,
Mum
x x x

I know it off by heart. I've made up a little tune and I sing it to myself every morning when I wake up and every night when I go to bed. I sing it softly in school. I sing it when I'm watching television. I sing it in the bath. I sing it on the toilet. I sing the punctuation and stuff too,

like: *'Christ-mas, question mark. Lots of love, comma, Mum, kiss kiss kiss.'* It's a very catchy tune. I might well be a song writer when I grow up as well as a famous novelist.

Of course I'm also going to be an actress just like my mum. I am soon going to be acclaimed as a brilliant child star. I have the ☆STAR☆ part in a major production this Christmas. Truly.

I am in our school's play of *A Christmas Carol.*

I haven't done too well in casting sessions in the past. At my other schools I never seemed to get picked for any really juicy roles. I was a donkey when we did a Nativity play. I was a little miffed that I wasn't Mary or the Angel Gabriel at the very least, but like a true little trooper I decided to make the most of my part.

I worked hard on developing authentic eeyore donkey noises. I eeyored like an entire herd of donkeys during the performance. OK, I maybe drowned out Mary's speech, and the Angel Gabriel's too (to say nothing of Joseph, the Innkeeper, the Three Wise Men and Assorted Shepherds), but real donkeys don't wait politely till people have finished talking, they eeyore whenever they feel like it. I felt like eeyoring constantly, so I did.

I didn't get picked to be in any more plays at that stupid old school. But this school's not too bad. We have a special art and drama teacher, Miss Simpkins. She understands that if we do art we need to be dead artistic and if we do drama then we should aim at being dead *dramatic*. She admired my arty paintings of Justine Littlewood being devoured by lions and tigers and bears.

'You're a very imaginative and lively girl, Tracy,' said Miss Simpkins.

I wasn't totally bowled over by this. That's the way social workers talk when they're trying to boost your confidence or sell you to prospective foster carers. 'Imaginative and lively' means you get up to all sorts of irritating and annoying tricks. *Me?* Well, maybe.

My famous imagination ran away with me when we were auditioning for *A Christmas Carol*. I didn't really know the story that well. It's ever so l-o-n-g and I'm a very busy person, with no time to read dull old books. Miss Simpkins gave us a quick précis version and I had a little fidget and yawn because it seemed so old fashioned and boring, but my ears pricked up – right out of my curls – when she said there were ghosts.

'I'll be a ghost, Miss. I'm great at scaring people. Look, look, I'm a headless ghost!' I pulled my school jumper up over my head and held my arms like claws and went, 'Whooooo!'

Silly little Peter Ingham squealed in terror and ducked under his desk.

'See, I can be really convincing, Miss! And I can do you all sorts of *different* ghosts. I can do your standard white-sheet spooky job, or I can moan and clank chains, or I could paint myself grey all over and

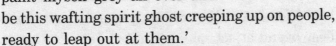

be this wafting spirit ghost creeping up on people, ready to leap out at them.'

I leaped out at Weedy Peter just as he emerged from under his desk. He shrieked and ducked, banging his head in the process.

'Well, you're certainly entering into the spirit

17

of things, Tracy,' said Miss Simpkins, bending down to rub Peter's head and give the little weed a cuddle. 'There now, Peter, don't look so scared. It isn't a real ghost, it's only Tracy Beaker.'

'I'm scared of Tracy Beaker,' said Peter. 'Even though she's my friend.'

I wish the little creep wouldn't go around telling everyone he's my friend. It's dead embarrassing. I don't want you to think he's my *only* friend. I've got heaps and heaps of friends. Well. Louise isn't my best friend any more. She's gone totally off her head because she now wants to be friends with Justine No-Fun-At-All Littlewood. There's no one in our class who actually quite measures up to my friendship requirements.

Hey, I *have* got a best friend. It's Cam! She comes to see me every Saturday. She's not like my mum, glamorous and beautiful and exciting. But she can sometimes be good fun. So she's my best friend. And Miss Simpkins can be my second best friend at school.

Peter's just my friend at the Dumping Ground. Especially at night time, when there's no one else around.

Peter seemed to be thinking about our night-

18

time get-togethers too.

'Promise promise promise you won't pretend to be a ghost tonight, Tracy?' he whispered anxiously.

'Ah! I'm afraid I can't possibly promise, Peter. I am the child of a famous Hollywood star. I take my acting seriously. I might well have to stay in character and act ghostly all the time,' I said.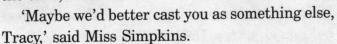

'Maybe we'd better cast you as something else, Tracy,' said Miss Simpkins.

'Oh no, *please* let me be the ghost!' I begged.

It turned out there were four main ghosts in *A Christmas Carol* and a motley crew of ghostly extras too.

There was the Ghost of Christmas Past.

'Let *me* be the Ghost of Christmas Past, Miss Simpkins,' I said.

Louise

'No, Tracy, I need a girl with long fair hair to be the Ghost of Christmas Past,' said Miss Simpkins.

She chose *Louise*.

'Now there's the Ghost of

19

Christmas Present,' said Miss Simpkins.

'Let *me* be the Ghost of Christmas Present,' I said.

'No, Tracy. I need a big jolly boy to be the Ghost of Christmas Present,' said Miss Simpkins.

She chose old Fatty Freddy.

'Now there's the Ghost of Christmas Yet to Come,' said Miss Simpkins.

Freddy

'I thought Charles Dickens was meant to be a good writer. He's a bit repetitive when it comes to ghosts, isn't he?' I said. 'Still, let *me* be the Ghost of Christmas Yet to Come.'

Philip

'No, Tracy, I need a very tall boy to be the Ghost of Christmas Yet to Come,' said Miss Simpkins.

She chose this pea-brained boy called Philip who couldn't haunt so much as a graveyard.

'There's just one more main ghost and that's Marley's Ghost,' said Miss Simpkins. 'He wails and clanks his chains.'

'Oooh, I'm a totally terrific wailer and clanker, you know I am! Let *me* be Marley's Ghost,' I begged.

'I'm very tempted, Tracy, but perhaps you might indulge in a tad too much wailing and clanking,' said Miss Simpkins.

Justine!

She chose *Justine Can't-Act-For-Toffee Littlewood*, who can't clank to save her life and can barely whimper, let alone give a good ghostly *wail*.

I was Severely Irritated with Miss Simpkins. I decided she wasn't my friend any more. I didn't want to be in her stupid play if she wouldn't pick me for one of the main ghosts. I didn't want to be one of the no-name *extra* ghosts or any of the other people – these silly Fezziwigs and Cratchits.

I turned my back on Miss Simpkins and whistled a festive tune to myself . . . with new lyrics.

'Jingle Bells, Miss Simpkins smells,
Jingle all the day.
Oh what a fart it is to take part
In her stupid Christmas play.'

21

'And now there's only one part left,' said Miss Simpkins. 'Are you listening to me, Tracy?'

I gave the tiniest shrug, slumping down in my seat. I tried to make it crystal clear that I wasn't remotely interested.

'I'll take that as a yes,' said Miss Simpkins cheerfully. 'Yes, there's just the part of crusty old Ebenezer Scrooge himself to cast. Now, I'm going to have serious problems. This is the key part of the whole play. The *best* part, the *leading* part. I need a consummate actor, one who isn't phased by a really big juicy part, one who can act bad temper and meanness and lack of generosity, and yet one who can convincingly thaw and repent and behave wonderfully after all. I wonder . . .'

I sat up straight. I gazed at Miss Simpkins. She surely couldn't mean . . .

'You, Tracy Beaker! You will be my Scrooge!' she said.

'Yay!' I shrieked. I bounced up and down in my seat as if I had an india-rubber bottom.

'That's stupid, Miss!' said Justine Can't-Hold-Her-Tongue Littlewood. 'You can't let Tracy be Scrooge. Why should she get the best part? She just mucks around and doesn't take things seriously. You can't let her be in the play, she'll just mess it up for all of us.'

'I'll certainly mess *you* up,' I mumbled.

I rushed out of my seat, right up to Miss Simpkins.

'I'll take it all dead seriously, Miss Simpkins, I promise. You can count on me. And don't be surprised if I turn out to be unexpectedly brilliant at acting as my mum is a Hollywood movie star making one film after another.'

'As if!' said Louise.

'I know the only sort of movies Tracy Beaker's mum would star in. *Blue* movies!' said Justine Liar-Liar-Liar Littlewood.

My fists clenched, I so badly wanted to punch her straight in the nose, but I knew she was just

23

trying to wind me up so Miss Simpkins would lose her temper with me and not let me be Scrooge after all. I simply raised my eyebrows and hissed a small rebuff along the lines that her dad belonged in a *horror* movie. Then I turned my back on her and smiled at Miss Simpkins.

'As I've got the biggest part you'd better give me a copy of the play straight away, Miss Simpkins, so I can get to be word perfect. In fact, maybe I ought to be excused all the boring lessons like literacy and maths just so I can concentrate on learning my part.'

'Nice try, Tracy, but I'm not that much of a pushover,' said Miss Simpkins. 'No, you'll have to learn your part in your own time.'

I was so anxious to play Scrooge I learned my lines in *other* people's time. Mostly Cam's. I used up two entire Saturday visits getting her to read out all the other parts while I Bah-Humbugged my way through Scrooge. Cam tried almost too hard at first, doing weird voices for all the Christmas ghosts and an extremely irritating little-boy lisp for Tiny Tim.

'Hey, *I'm* the one that's supposed to be acting, not you,' I said. 'Just *speak* the lines.'

'Look, I'm the adult. Aren't I the one supposed to tell *you* what to do?' said Cam, swatting me with the script of the play. 'Oh no, sorry, I forgot. You're Tracy Beaker so you get to be Big Bossy-Knickers, right?'

'Absolutely right, Cam. You got it in one! Hey, all this saying lines about sucking pigs and sausages has made me simply starving. Any chance of us going out to McDonald's?'

Mike

Jenny

I didn't just pester Cam to hear my lines. I got Jenny and Mike at the Dumping Ground to help me out, though I got dead annoyed when they wanted Justine Utter-Rubbish Littlewood and Louise and weedy little Peter to attend our special rehearsals too.

'It's not fair! I can't concentrate with all that rabble around,' I declared. 'Let's send them packing.'

'They're all in *A Christmas Carol* too, Tracy. You're not the only one who needs help with your lines,' said Jenny.

'We can act it all out together,' said Mike. 'Trust you to behave like a prima donna, Tracy.'

'Yeah, trust me, because what is the definition of prima donna, Mike? Isn't she the star of the whole show? I rest my case!'

I even considered commandeering Elaine the Pain to help me with my part. She's always encouraging us looked-after kids to role-play and act out our angst so I wondered if she might have any useful tips.

I'd lost it a little there. As if Old Elaine could

ever be useful at anything! Especially Elaine in Christmas mode, decking our ropy Dumping Ground with tinsel and home-made paper chains, a pair of wacky rainbow antlers bobbing manically on her head and a Comic Relief nose pinching her own. She was wearing a holly-berry-red knitted jumper and an ivy-green skirt, way too tight, and was warbling the words of 'Rudolph the Red-nosed Reindeer'.

'Elaine my social worker
Had a very large fat bum,
And if you ever saw her
You would scream out loud and run,'
I sang under my breath.

Not quite under enough. Elaine heard and got quite aerated. She burbled on about Cheek and Attitude and Silly Offensive Personal Remarks that could be Really Hurtful. I started to feel a little bit mean. I was even considering saying sorry. Elaine can't *help* having a huge bum after all.

27

She said she understood I was feeling tense and anxious because she'd heard I'd taken on a huge part in our school play when I simply wasn't used to Applying Myself and Being Responsible.

I stopped feeling even the tiniest bit sorry. I was glad when I heard Elaine say to Jenny, 'Look, can I ask you for a really honest answer? Do you think my bu— behind looks a bit big in my new skirt?'

I decided I would simply rely on myself and learn my part properly and show them all. This was fine and dandy during the day but not quite so easy at night. I kept having these bizarre nightmares where I was all alone on stage and I kept opening my mouth like a goldfish but no sound at all came out. I couldn't so much as blow a bubble. The audience started getting restless, pelting me with rotten fruit. One maggoty old apple landed straight in my gaping mouth, so I looked exactly like the Ghost of Christmas Present's sucking pig.

Then they put me on a spit and roasted me. I screamed that I was burning so they threw water at me. Lots and lots of water . . . When I woke up my bed was unaccountably wet and I had to go on a dismal damp trek to the bathroom and the linen cupboard.

I met up with Weedy Peter on a similar mission. He was actually crying. Like I said, I never cry. I might occasionally have an attack of hay fever but that is a medical condition, not an emotional state.

'What are you blubbing for, silly?' I asked.

'I'm so scared I'll be rubbish in the school Christmas play,' Peter sobbed. 'I wish wish wish Miss Simpkins hadn't made me be Tiny Tim. I don't *want* to act. I can't remember the words and I can't figure out which leg to hop on, and it will all be so so so much worse with people watching us. It's all right for you, Tracy. You never get scared of anything and you're a terrible show-off so acting's right up your street.'

'Cheek! Don't you dare call me a terrible show-off!' I said.

'But you are.'

'Yes, I know, but you don't have to point it out.'

'I'd give *anything* to be a terrible show-off,' Peter said earnestly. 'Can't you show me how, Tracy? Is there a special trick?'

'It's just a natural gift, Peter,' I said. 'I was born showing off. I shot out of my mum and said, "Hi, folks!" to the doctor and the nurse, and then I turned a somersault, stood on my tiny feet and did a little tap dance on the delivery table.'

I felt for Peter's head in the dark. His mouth was hanging open. I closed it gently.

'Joke,' I said. 'OK, as an extra special favour to you, Peter, we'll act out all our scenes together.'

We started meeting up for midnight rehearsals on a regular basis. Peter was soon word perfect because he had hardly any lines to learn. I mean, how hard is it to remember 'God bless us, every one' for goodness sake? But though he could say the words he couldn't *act* them at all. He just mumbled them in a monotone.

'You certainly *are* rubbish at acting, Peter,' I said. 'Oh stop it, don't go all sniffly on me. I'm not being mean, I'm simply stating a fact. But don't worry, I'll help. You've got to feel your way into the part. You're this little weedy boy with a delicate constitution and a gammy leg. That's not hard, is it? Talk about type-casting.'

'I haven't got a gammy leg,' said Peter the Pedant.

'I'll kick it hard if you like,' I said. 'Now, even though you're down on your luck, you're a chirpy little soul, the favourite of your family. Your dad especially dotes on you.'

'I wish that bit was true,' said Peter mournfully.

'Yeah. Me too,' I said.

We huddled closer under our shared blanket.

'I wish I had a family to come and see me in the play,' said Peter. 'Well, maybe I don't – not if I'm rubbish.'

'You won't be rubbish, you'll be terrific with the

Totally Tremendous Tracy Beaker directing you.
Yes, it's sad you haven't got anyone. Never mind,
I'll ask my mum to give you a special wave.'

'Your mum's coming?' Peter asked, sounding
astonished.

'You bet. She's coming for Christmas, she
promised,' I said. 'She'll be desperate to watch
me act to see if I've inherited her show-biz talents
– which I *have*. I've written her a letter telling
her all about the show.'

I'd written her several letters. In fact I wrote
to her every single day and gave them to Jenny
to post.

Dear Mum,

I can't wait to see you at Christmas,
remember, you promised? Can you come
a week early so you can come to my school
play and see me in my {STAR} role as
Scrooge? I am dead good at being a mean
miserable old man.

Lots and lots and lots of love from
your happy cheery little daughter

Tracy xxx

'I know just how much you want to see your mum, Tracy, but don't get *too* fixated on her coming to see you,' said Elaine.

'But she is, she wrote and said – she promised . . . practically.'

'I know how much you want her to come, but sometimes our wishes don't always come true,' said Elaine.

I wished I didn't have a social worker. I wished I had a fairy godmother who said, 'You want your mum to come and see you? Certainly, Tracy, no problem,' and she'd wave her wand and *wow! pow!* there would be my mum, all pink and powdery and perfect, her arms outstretched ready to give me a big hug.

I haven't got a fairy godmother. I have to work my own magic.

The next Saturday Cam came to see me at the Dumping Ground as usual. We had a quick run-through of the whole play – and I mean *quick*. I gabbled my way through my part like I was on fast forward. I possibly missed out whole chunks, but when Cam pointed this out I just said, 'Yeah, yeah, whatever, but I'm on *this* bit now,' and revved up into Thousand-Words-A-Minute Top Gear.

We finished the play in twenty minutes dead.

'Right! Done the rehearsal. Now let's go out,' I said.

'Ah! So McDonald's is calling?' said Cam.

'No. Well, *yes*, I'm starving actually, but I want to go round the shops. I want to do some Christmas shopping.'

Jenny gives all of us older kids a special Christmas shopping allowance. She goes shopping with the little kids and helps them choose – otherwise they just spend it on sweets for themselves. Us older kids usually snaffle a little for sweets too, but this time I wanted *all* my money for presents. One set of presents in particular.

'I might as well do my Christmas shopping too, Tracy,' said Cam.

'Ooh! What are you getting for me, Cam?' I asked, momentarily diverted. 'I could really do with some new jeans. Designer, natch. And one of those really cool furry jackets with a hood. And there's this seriously wicked motorized go-cart that would be fun for swooping all round the gardens of the Dumping Ground – *swoosh*, *swoosh* – Oh I'm *sorry*, Justine Littlewood, was that your foot?'

'Tracy, I can't afford to buy you so much as a motorized matchbox at the moment. I'm totally skint. You've got to adopt a new attitude. *It's the thought that counts.*'

'It strikes me *you* should be playing Scrooge, not me, if you're not giving proper Christmas presents,' I said. 'Honestly, Cam, why don't you get your act together and write a socking great bestseller? Something that would be snapped up by Hollywood in a million-dollar movie deal. Then me and my mum could star in it.'

'Dream on, sweetheart,' said Cam. 'I somehow don't think I'm bestseller material.'

'You've got to think positive, Cam. You've got to *make* your dreams come true,' I said.

I was intent on doing just that.

When we got to the shopping centre I got Cam to come to Boots with me to buy some really special make-up.

'So what's the *best* brand, Cam?' I asked.

'Don't ask me, Tracy, I hardly ever wear make-up. I just buy whatever's cheapest,' she said.

'Well, this is a present for my mum so I want the most glamorous gorgeous stuff possible.'

I fiddled around trying out different lipstick shades on my wrist until it looked like I had red-rose tattoos up both arms.

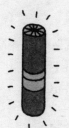

Then I finally selected the most perfect pearly pink.

Cam thought we were done.

'No, no! Hand lotion next!'

Cam sighed and fidgeted while I tried out all the lotions, sniffing them carefully and comparing them for creaminess. After a while my hands got very slippery and sticky and I had to wipe them on my skirt.

'I don't think Jenny's going to be very thrilled about those great greasy marks,' said Cam. 'Come *on*, Tracy, let's go to the bookshop now.'

'No, no, I've got to get my mum another present. I need a jewellery shop now.'

'But you've already got your mum the lipstick *and* the hand lotion.' Cam sneaked a peek in my purse. 'Don't forget you've got to buy Christmas presents for everyone.'

I wasn't interested in buying presents for everyone. I didn't want to buy a present for anyone but my *mum*.

I dragged Cam into a lovely sparkly jewellery shop, but when I saw the prices of even the weeniest rings I had to back away, sighing.

'That's real jewellery, Tracy. A little bit ostentatious, all that gold and diamonds. I think costume jewellery is much more tasteful,' Cam said quickly.

'OK. Where do you buy this costume jewellery then?'

She took me to the ground floor of this big department store and I walked round and round great glass cabinets of jewellery. I saw a pink heart on a crimson ribbon. It was utterly beautiful. I could just imagine it round my mum's neck. It was *very* expensive, even for costume jewellery, but I counted out every last penny in my purse and found I could just about manage it, keeping a fiver back for my last-of-all purchase.

'Are you *sure*, Tracy? I think maybe your mum would be happy with just the lipstick. Or the hand lotion.'

'My mum likes *lots* of presents,' I said. 'I know what I'm doing, Cam.'

I *didn't* really know what I was going to do about everyone else's presents. Still, I wasn't speaking to Louise any more on account of the

38

fact she'd ganged up with Justine Ugly-Unscrupulous-Friend-Snatcher Littlewood so I didn't have to buy her anything.

There was Jenny and Mike, but they quite liked all that pathetic home-made calendar and dried-pasta-picture rubbish. Maybe Miss Simpkins at school would go for that sort of stuff too. Ditto Cam. She believed that it was the thought that counted, didn't she? She'd as good as indicated that I wasn't getting anything to speak of from her. It would only embarrass her if I gave her too lavish a gift.

That just left Weedy Peter. I was sure I could fob him off with something of mine I didn't want any more, like my leather wallet with the broken clasp or my leaky snowstorm or my wrinkly copy of *The Lion, the Witch and the Wardrobe* that got a little damp when I was reading it in the bath.

I heaved a sigh of relief. Christmas-present problem *sorted*. Now there was just one present left.

'Come on, Cam, I've got to go to a bookshop,' I said, tugging her.

She was peering at some very boring pearls in the jewellery cabinet.

'Bookshop! Now we're talking. But hang on. Look, what do you think of that little pearl necklace there – the one with the diamanté clasp? All the sparkly stuff's half price, special offer.'

'Cam, you are so *not* a pearl necklace person.'

'They're not for me, silly.'

I blinked at her. 'Look, Cam, it's very kind of you, but actually *I'm* not a pearl necklace person either.'

Cam snorted. 'You can say that again, Tracy. No no no, I'm thinking about my mum.'

'Ah. Yes. She's quite posh, isn't she, your mum?'

'Insufferably so. Very very much a pearl sort of person. But *real* pearls. These are fake so I expect she'd turn her nose up at them.'

'Well, get her real ones then.'

'Don't be a banana, Tracy. I couldn't possibly afford them. I can't actually afford the fake ones, even half price. You know, I'm like a fake

40

daughter to my mum. She's *so* disappointed that I'm not all smart and glossy with a posh partner and a brilliant career.'

'Well, you could still try to get them,' I said doubtfully.

'I don't want to. I want to be *me*. It's so hard not to get wound up by my mum. I'm absolutely dreading going home for Christmas.'

'You're *dreading* going home for Christmas?' I said slowly.

Cam stopped gazing at the fake pearls and looked at me.

'Oh Tracy, I'm sorry. That was such a stupid tactless thing to say to you. I know just how much you want to see your mum this Christmas.'

'And I'm going to,' I said, very firmly and fiercely.

'Well, that would be truly great, but remember, your mum might just be busy or tied up or . . . or . . . abroad,' Cam said.

'No, she's going to be here. She's going to come and see me in my starring role in *A Christmas Carol*. And then she'll stay over. I dare say she'll take us to this top hotel and we'll have Christmas there. Yeah, it will be so great. We'll sleep in this big big queen-size bed and then we'll splash in our power shower and then we'll have the most immense breakfast. I'll be allowed to eat whatever I want. I can put six spoonfuls of sugar on my cereal and eat twenty sausages in one go and I'll have those puffy things with maple syrup—'

'Waffles?'

'Yeah, I'll scoffle a waffle,' I said as we walked out of the department store towards the bookshop. 'I'll scoffle *six* waffles and I'll have hot chocolate with whipped cream, and *then* I'll open my presents and my mum will give me heaps and heaps and heaps of stuff – a whole wardrobe of designer clothes, enough new shoes and trainers and boots to shod a giant centipede—'

'And a motorized go-cart? Sorry, a whole *fleet* of them.'

'Yep, and bikes and scooters and my own trampoline, and I'll be able to bounce soooo high I'll swoop straight up to the sky and everyone will look up at me and go, *Is it a bird? Is it a plane? Is it Superman? Is it Santa? Noooo, it's the Truly Tremendous Tracy Beaker!*'

I bounced up and down to demonstrate. I accidentally landed on Cam's foot and she gave a little scream, but she was very nice about it.

We carried on playing the Christmas game until we got to the bookshop. Well, it wasn't exactly a game. I knew it was all going to come true, though perhaps I was embellishing things a little. I am occasionally prone to exaggeration. That means I can get carried away and tell socking great lies. They start to seem so real that I believe them too.

Cam was very happy to be in the bookshop. She ran her finger lovingly along the long lines of paperbacks.

'I'll have a little browse,' she said. 'The children's section is over in that corner, Tracy.'

'I don't want the children's books. I want the classics section,' I said loftily.

'Oh yes?' said Cam. 'You fancy a quick flick through *War and Peace*?'

'That's quite a good title. If I write my true life story about my Dumping Ground experiences I'll call my book *War and More War and Yet More War*. No, I'm going to peruse the collected works of Mr Charles Dickens.'

That showed her. I wasn't kidding either. I wanted to find a copy of *A Christmas Carol*. I found a very nice paperback for £4.99. I had just one penny left. I didn't put it back in my purse. I decided to throw it in the dinky wishing well by the shopping centre Christmas tree.

I could do with a good wishing session.

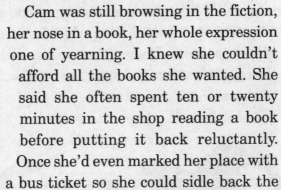

Cam was still browsing in the fiction, her nose in a book, her whole expression one of yearning. I knew she couldn't afford all the books she wanted. She said she often spent ten or twenty minutes in the shop reading a book before putting it back reluctantly. Once she'd even marked her place with a bus ticket so she could sidle back the next day – and the next and the next and the next – until she'd finished the whole story.

I suddenly wished I'd saved just a little bit of my Christmas money to buy Cam a paperback. I fidgeted uncomfortably with my wishing penny. I threw it up and caught it again and again, practising my wishing. Then I dropped it and it rolled off, right round the shelves. I ran after it and practically bumped my nose on the MIND BODY SPIRIT sign.

I picked up my penny, my eyes glazing over at all these dippy books about star signs and spiritual auras – and then I saw a title in sparkly silver lettering: *Make Your Wishes Come True*.

45

I reached for the book, my hand shaking. It was a slim little book, written by someone called Grizelda Moonbeam, White Witch. I considered calling myself Tracy Moonbeam, Very Black Witch. I'd learn magic spells and make frogs and toads spew out of Justine Get-Everyone-On-Her-Side Littlewood.

I opened the book and started flipping through the pages. It really was full of spells! I couldn't find a frog-and-toad curse for your worst enemy, but there were plenty of love potions and magic charms. I turned another page and then my heart started thumping.

'CHARM TO BE WITH YOUR LOVED ONE ON A FESTIVE OCCASION'.

My mum was my Very Much Loved One and you couldn't get a more Festive Occasion than Christmas. I so badly wanted her to come this Christmas and watch me act Scrooge on stage I was about ready to pop.

I read the charm carefully. Grizelda advised mixing one part mead to two parts dandelion wine, adding cinnamon for spice and ginger for warmth and sugar for  sweetness. She suggested stirring the mixture well while chanting the Loved One's name, then drinking from the wrong side of the glass without drawing breath.

I blinked. Easy-peasy! I gabbled the ingredients over and over again. I'd got so used to learning my Scrooge lines that the recipe tucked itself neatly inside my head without too much fussing. Then I reverently replaced Grizelda Moonbeam, danced seven times around the bookshelf because it seemed a magic thing to do, and then staggered giddily off to find Cam.

'Are you feeling OK, Tracy?' she asked, as I bumped right into her.

'I'm fine,' I said, carefully sorting out my carrier bags *and* my penny. 'Come on, Cam, let's get cracking. I've got all my Christmas presents now.'

'And I haven't got a sausage,' said Cam, sighing. 'Oh well, maybe I can make some of my presents this year.'

I shook my head at her. 'Look, Cam, making presents is for little kids. *I* can barely get away with it. You're way too old, believe me. And forget *all* about it on my behalf. I want a proper present!'

'You don't really work hard to get people to like you, Tracy,' said Cam, shutting her book with a snap.

'I don't have to. I'm bubbling over with natural charm,' I said.

However, I pondered her point as we left the bookshop. What *was* all this gubbins about getting people to like you? I didn't fancy sucking up to people all the time and saying they looked lovely when they looked rubbish and all that sick-making nonsense. Louise was a past master at that – and a present mistress too. She could flutter her long eyelashes, fix you with a

48

soulful glance with her big blue eyes and say softly that you were the funniest girl in all the world and she wanted to be your best friend for ever and you actually *believed* it, until she ganged up with Someone Else.

Still, I wouldn't want to be Louise's best friend any more. I don't *want* her to like me again. I definitely don't want Justine Dog-Breath-Snake-Tongue-Baboon-Bottom Littlewood to like me.

I don't need to work at getting people to like me. Heaps and heaps of people do. I go out of my way to *stop* Weedy Peter liking me. Elaine and Jenny and Mike like me too. They do heaps of things for me, don't they? Although they're paid to hang out with me. Maybe they simply can't stick me but don't tell me because it would be unprofessional.

It was silly thinking like this. I was starting to panic. It wasn't good for me to get so worked up, though of course all great actors were hypersensitive and temperamental. Miss Simpkins liked me or she wouldn't have offered me the starring part in her play. Unless . . . she was simply sorry for me because I was little Tracy No-Friends, the most unpopular girl in the whole school.

Maybe Cam didn't like me either. She just came to take me out every week as a duty. She was making a fuss of the Sad Ugly Kid with Mega Attitude Problems because it made her feel good. Maybe I was her Unpleasant Weekly Project, on a par with taking out the rubbish and cleaning the toilet.

'Tracy? Why are you breathing all funny?' said Cam, as we walked through the shopping centre.

'I'm hyperventilating on account of your hostile remarks,' I said, going extra gaspy to give her a fright.

'What do you mean?'

'You said no one likes me,' I said.

I suddenly couldn't *help* gasping I felt so horrible.

'I *didn't*!' Cam said.

'You did, you did, you did, and it's outrageous to say that to a looked-after child. You've probably traumatized me for life,' I said, giving her a shove.

I used my elbows and they're particularly sharp.

'Ouch! You've probably *punctured* me for life with your stiletto elbows.'

'Well, I'm fading away with hunger. It's no wonder I'm so skinny. You'd better whip me to McDonald's quick, what with my general anorexic state and my tragic realization that everyone totally hates me.'

'Oh Tracy, will you just *stop* it. I didn't say anyone hated you. I didn't say anyone didn't like you. I simply said you didn't try hard to make people like you.' Cam paused. She took hold of me by the shoulders, staring straight into my eyes. 'But even when you treat me like dirt *I* still like you.'

I relaxed.

'Mind you, I'd like you even more if you'd try being gentle and considerate and polite,' said Cam.

'*Me?*' I said. 'Dream on! Come on, I want my Big Mac and fries. Please. Dear kind pretty ever-so-nice-to-me Camilla.'

'Yuck! It was working till you said my name.

That's what my mum calls me. Oh God, I wish it wasn't nearly Christmas.'

I had my own wish to make. A real magic spell, *much* more powerful than throwing a penny in a polystyrene wishing well. I went over it in my head as I munched my burger and gobbled my chips and slurped my shake.

'Can we go back to your house for tea, Cam?' I asked. 'Hey, I've thought what I want for tea too.'

'You're only just having your lunch, girl.'

'Yeah, yeah, but I want something *special* for tea. Something Christmasy.'

'You know I'm pretty skint at the moment. I expect I can manage a sausage on a stick and a mince pie but that's about my limit.'

'Never mind that stuff. Well, yes to sausages and yes to mince pies too, and a chocolate log would be a good idea, come to think of it, but what I was really hoping for was Christmas punch.'

'What?'

'You know. A special festive drink. There's this amazing punch I've heard about. You mix one part mead to two parts dandelion wine, and then you add cinnamon and ginger and sugar, stir it all around, and Bob's your uncle, Fanny's your aunt, yummy yummy in your tummy.' I mimed being a cocktail barman for her and ended up with a flourish.

'Cheers!' I said, raising my imaginary glass.

Cam blinked at me. 'Well, personally I prefer a simple glass of wine as a festive drink, but each to their own. We can try and fix you something similar—'

'No, no, you can't muck about with the ingredients, it'll lose all its potency,' I said urgently.

Cam's eyes narrowed. 'Tracy, have you taken up witchcraft?'

She is so spooky at times. It's as if she can open a little flap in my head and peer straight into my mind.

'Watch out if I *am* a trainee witch, Cam. Think of the havoc I could wreak,' I said, contorting my face into a witchy grimace and making manic old-hag cackles.

'Help help help,' said Cam, raising her

eyebrows. 'OK, I'll see what we can do. Come on, let's have a trek round Sainsbury's and see what we can come up with.'

We couldn't find any mead at all *or* dandelion wine. I started to fuss considerably.

'It's OK, Tracy. Mead is a honey drink,' Cam told me. 'I've got a jar of honey at home so we'll put a spoonful of honey in a glass of wine, and pick a dandelion on the way home and chop it up and add it too, OK? I've got sugar and we'll buy a little pot of cinnamon and – what was the other thing? Oh, ginger. Well, I think I've got a packet of ginger biscuits somewhere. They might be a bit stale but I don't suppose that matters.'

I was still a bit doubtful. I wanted to do it all *properly* but it couldn't be helped. When we got back to Cam's I carefully washed the dandelion leaf. It had been very hard to find. Cam eventually reached through the slats of someone's gate and picked a plant from their front garden.

'Um!' I said. 'Isn't that stealing?'

'It's weeding,' said Cam firmly. 'Dandelions are weeds.'

'If that *is* a dandelion.'

'Of course it is, Tracy.'

'What do you know about plants, Cam?'

'Look, I might not be Alan Titchmarsh, but I know my dandelions from my dock leaves. That is a dandelion, OK? So get chopping.'

I chopped the dandelion into little green specks, I crumbled the biscuits and spooned out the honey and sugar. Cam poured some wine into her prettiest pink wine glass. She lifted it absent-mindedly to her lips.

'Hey, hey, it's *my* potion!' I said.

'OK, OK,' said Cam, sighing. 'Go on then, shove the rest of the stuff in – though it seems a shame to muck up a perfectly good glass of wine.'

'This isn't a *drink*, Cam. It's a potion. *My* potion,' I said. 'Now, let me sprinkle and stir. You keep quiet. I have to concentrate.'

I concentrated like crazy, sprinkling in every little green dandelion speck and the ginger and the sugar and the honey, and then I stirred it vigorously with a spoon.

'Hey, gently with that glass!' said Cam.

'Shh! And don't listen to me, this is *private*,' I hissed. I took a deep breath. 'Please work, charm,' I muttered. 'Let me be with my Loved One on a Festive Occasion – i.e. this Christmas! I need her there to see me in *A Christmas Carol* and then I want her to stay so we have the best Christmas ever together.'

Then I raised the glass, stuck my chin in to reach the wrong side and took a gulp of wine without drawing breath. It tasted *disgusting*, but I swallowed it down determinedly, wishing and wishing to make it come true.

'Steady on, Tracy! Don't drink it all – you'll get drunk!' said Cam.

I didn't want to break the spell so I ignored her. I took another gulp and then spluttered and choked. The potion went up my nose and then snorted back out of it in totally disgusting fashion. I gasped while Cam patted me on the back and mopped me with a tissue.

'Oh dear, have I mucked up the magic?' I wheezed.

'No, no, you absorbed the potion through extra orifices so I guess that makes it even more potent,' said Cam. 'Still, seriously, no more! Jenny would never forgive me if I took you back to the Home totally blotto.'

'Oh gosh, Cam, I think I *am* utterly totally sloshed out of my skull,' I slurred, reeling around, pretending to trip and stumble.

'Tracy!' said Cam, rushing to catch me.

'Only joking!' I giggled.

'Well, maybe I'd better have a swig too if it's as potent as that,' said Cam. She took the spoon and stirred it around herself, and then she mouthed something before she took a sip, drinking from the wrong side of the glass without drawing breath. Then she choked too, dribbling all down her chin.

It was my turn to clap her on the back.

'Hey, gently, Tracy!' Cam spluttered. 'Oh God. It tastes revolting. What a waste of wine.

Let's hope it jolly well works for both of us.'

'So who is *your* Loved One?' I said.

I wasn't too happy about this. As far as I knew Cam didn't have any Loved Ones, and that suited me just fine. I didn't want some bloke commandeering her on Saturdays and mucking up our special days together.

I knew what blokes could be like. That's how I started off in Care. My mum got this awful Monster Gorilla Boyfriend and he was horrible to me so I had to be taken away. I'd just like to see him try now. I was only little then. Well, I'm still quite little now but I am Incredibly Fierce and a Ferocious Fighter. Just ask Justine Bashed-To-A-Pulp Littlewood. If I encountered Monster Gorilla Boyfriend *now* I'd karate-chop him and then I'd kick him downstairs, out of the door, out of my life.

If Cam's anonymous Loved One started any funny business then he'd definitely get treated the same way. Beware the Beaker Boyfriend Deterrent!

'You haven't got a boyfriend, have you, Cam?' I asked her, as she fixed me a fruit smoothie to take away the terrible taste of the potion.

'A boyfriend?' said Cam, looking reassuringly surprised. 'Oh Tracy, don't *you* start. My mum always goes on at me whenever I see her.' She put on this piercing posh voice. *'Haven't you met any decent men yet, Camilla? Mind you, I'm not surprised no one's interested. Look at the state of you – that terrible short haircut and those wretched jeans!'*

Cam poured herself a glass of wine and took several sips. 'Oh dear. Shut me up whenever I get onto the subject of my mum.' She shuddered dramatically. 'OK, how's about trying a plateful of cinnamon toast?'

It was utterly yummy. I had six slices. I didn't get Cam's mum-phobia. I *love* talking about my mum. But then I've got the best and most beautiful movie-star actress for a mum. Maybe I wouldn't be anywhere near as keen if I had a snobby old bag for a mum like Cam.

I usually hate it when Cam takes me back to the Dumping Ground but I was quite cool about it this evening because I had Mega Things to Do. I raided Elaine's art therapy cupboard (I'm ace at picking locks) and helped myself to lots of bright pink tissue paper and the best thin white card and a set of halfway-decent felt-tip pens.

It wasn't really *stealing*. I was using them for dead artistic and extremely therapeutic purposes.

I shoved my art materials up my jumper and shuffled my way up to my room and then proceeded to be Creative.

I was still actively Creating when Jenny knocked on my door. She tried to come in but she couldn't, on account of the fact that I'd shoved my chair hard against it to repel all intruders.

'What are you up to in there, Tracy? Let me in!'

'Do you mind, Jenny? I'm working on something dead secret.'

'That's what I was afraid of! What are you doing? I want to see.'

'No, you mustn't look. I'm making Christmas presents,' I hissed.

'Ah!' said Jenny. 'Oh, Tracy, how lovely. I'm sorry, sweetheart, I'll leave you alone. But it's getting late. Switch your light out soon, pet.'

She went off down the corridor humming 'Jingle Bells', obviously thinking I was making *her* Christmas present. I'd have to get cracking now and make her something. Ditto Mike. Ditto Elaine. And ditto Cam, of course, though I would have liked to give her a proper present. Still, I had to have my priorities. Mum came first.

I wrapped the lipstick in pink tissue. Then I cut out a rectangle from the cardboard, drew a pair of smiley pink lips and carefully printed in tiny neat letters:

YOU WILL SMILE WITH SHINY LIPS
WHEN YOU SEE ME ACT SCROOGE
IN 'A CHRISTMAS CAROL',
7 PM WEDNESDAY 20 DECEMBER
AT KINGLEA JUNIOR SCHOOL!!!

I stuck the label on the first packet and then made three more. I drew two hands on the second label and printed:

YOU WILL CLAP TILL YOUR HANDS
ARE SORE WHEN YOU WATCH ME
AS SCROOGE IN 'A CHRISTMAS CAROL'
7 PM WEDNESDAY 20 DECEMBER
AT KINGLEA JUNIOR SCHOOL !!!

I stuck this label on the wrapped hand lotion.
On the *third* label I drew a big pulsing heart and printed:

YOUR HEART WILL THUMP WITH
PRIDE WHEN YOU SEE ME ACT SCROOGE
IN 'A CHRISTMAS CAROL'
7 PM WEDNESDAY 20 DECEMBER
AT KINGLEA JUNIOR SCHOOL !!!

Then I wrapped up the beautiful heart necklace, taking care not to twist the red ribbon, and stuck the label on the pink tissue parcel.

Three presents wrapped and labelled. Just one to go! It took the longest though, because I had to annotate the book of *A Christmas Carol*. I drew me dressed up as Scrooge inside the front cover, with a special bubble saying, '*Bah! Humbug!*' I drew me dressed up as Scrooge inside the back cover too, but this time I was taking a bow at the end of my performance. There were lots of clapping hands and speech bubbles saying HURRAY! and MAGNIFICENT! and WELL DONE, TRACY! and THE GREATEST PERFORMANCE EVER! and A TRUE STAR IS BORN!

BAH! HUMBUG!

I wrote on the title page:

You don't have to read all this book,
You just have to come and watch me act
Scrooge in 'A Christmas Carol', 7pm on
Wednesday 20 December at Kinglea
Junior School !!! I will dedicate my
performance to YOU, the best mum in
the whole world ever.

All my love
Tracy xxxxxxxx

Then I wrapped *A Christmas Carol* and worked on the last label. I drew the book, scrunching up the title really small so it would fit, and underneath I printed:

THIS IS A GREAT BOOK AND IT'S BEEN TURNED INTO A GREAT PLAY AND THE GREATEST PART IS SCROOGE AND I AM PLAYING HIM (7PM ON WEDNESDAY 20 DECEMBER AT KINGLEA JUNIOR SCHOOL) SO PLEASE PLEASE PLEASE COME AND WATCH ME! ALL MY LOVE Tracy xxxxxxxxx

Then I sat for a long time holding all four pink parcels on my lap, imagining my mum opening them and putting on her lipstick, rubbing in her hand lotion, fastening the heart necklace, looking at the messages in the book. I imagined her jumping in her car and driving directly to see her superstar daughter. She'd be so proud of me she'd never ever want to go away without me.

KINGLEA 20m

The next morning I cornered Jenny in her office and asked if she had a big Jiffy bag so I could send my presents to my mum.

'It's a little bit early to send your Christmas presents, isn't it, Tracy?' Jenny said.

'No, no, these are *before* Christmas presents,' I said. 'We have to send them off first thing on Monday morning. First class.'

'OK. First thing, first class. I suppose *I'm* paying the postage?' said Jenny.

'Yes, and can you write on the Jiffy bag *Urgent!*

Open Immediately! Look, maybe *I'd* better do it,' I said.

'I think I can manage that, Tracy,' said Jenny.

'You are sure you've got my mum's right address?' I asked anxiously.

They don't let me have

it now on account of the fact that I tried to run away to find her. They won't let me have her phone number either. It is bitterly unfair, seeing as she's *my* mother. I have had major mega strops about it, but they won't give in.

'Don't worry, Tracy, I've got your mum's address,' said Jenny.

'It's just that it's ultra important. I need her to come and see me in the school play,' I said.

'I'm so glad you've been picked for the play, Tracy. You will take it seriously, won't you? No messing around or you'll spoil it for everyone.'

'Of course I'm taking it seriously, Jenny,' I said, insulted.

I was taking it very very very seriously – unlike *some* people. We had a play rehearsal every lunch time and half the kids mucked about and ate their sandwiches as they mumbled their lines. The carol singers sang off-key and the extra ghosts whimpered rather than wailed and the dancers kept bumping into each other and Weedy Peter kept forgetting his lines. He even forgot which was his lame leg, limping first on his left leg and then on his right.

'You are just so totally useless, Peter. How can you *possibly* keep forgetting "God bless us every one"?' said Justine Big-Mouth Littlewood. She seized hold of him and made like she was peering into his ear. 'Yes, just as I thought. You've not got any brain at all. It's just empty space inside your niddy-noddy head.'

I was thinking on similar lines myself, but when I saw poor Peter's face crumple I felt furious with her.

'You leave Peter alone, Justine Great-Big-Bully Littlewood. He's doing just fine – unlike you! I've never seen such a pathetic ghost in all my life. You're meant to be spooky but you couldn't scare so much as a sausage.'

Miss Simpkins clapped her hands. 'Hey, hey, girls! Calm down now. Concentrate on the play,' she said. 'Justine, you could put a little more *effort* into your Marley portrayal. Tracy, maybe you could try a little *less*. You're a splendid Scrooge but you don't need to furrow your brow and scowl *quite* so ferociously, and I think spitting at people when you say

"Bah! Humbug!" is a little too emphatic, plus I don't think the caretaker would approve of you dribbling all over the stage.'

'I'm simply getting under the skin of my character, Miss Simpkins,' I said.

She wasn't listening. She was busy shepherding the spare ghosts into a haunting formation.

'Yeah, you get under everyone's skin, Tracy Beaker,' hissed Justine Make-No-Effort-At-All Littlewood. 'You're like a big pus-y pimple.'

Louise giggled. 'Watch out or we'll squeeze you!' she said.

I gave her a shove. She shoved me back. Justine shoved too, harder. I was a bit off balance, hunched up in crabbed Scrooge mode. I ended up on my bottom.

They laughed. I tried not to cry because it hurt so much. Not that I ever cry, of course.

But sudden shocks to my system occasionally bring on an attack of my hay fever. It wasn't just bumping my bum. It was the fact that Louise was being so horrible. I was used to Justine Mean-Mouth Littlewood being foul to me, but it was so unfair that Louise was ganging up with her against me.

Louise had always been *my* friend. Now I didn't have any friend at all apart from Weedy Peter, and he barely counted.

'She's *crying*! You baby!' said Justine Mockingbird-Big-Beak Littlewood.

'Why don't you fight back, Tracy?' said Louise, looking uncomfortable.

'She's lost her bottle,' said Justine Hateful-Pig Littlewood. 'Boo-hoo, boo-hoo, baby! Does little diddums wants her mumsy to kiss it better? Only dream on, diddums, cause Mumsy isn't ever ever ever going to come.'

'I'll show you if I've lost my bottle,' I said, struggling to my feet.

I went *push punch whack kick!* Justine reeled backwards, her big nose all bloody after intimate contact with my fist.

Mrs Darlow

At that precise moment Mrs Darlow the headteacher came through the swing doors to see how the Christmas play was progressing. For a split second we were all stopped in our tracks, as if we'd been Paused. Then we were Fast Forwarded into alarming and ear-splitting action.

Justine started screaming. Louise did too, though I didn't even touch her. Peter started wailing. Some of the little kid dancers and carol singers started whimpering. Miss Simpkins looked like she wanted to burst into tears too.

She rushed over to Justine and picked her up and peered at her bloody nose.

Mrs Darlow marched over to me, snorting through *her* nose. 'Tracy Beaker, how dare you attack another pupil! How many times have I got to tell you that I will *not* have fighting in my school?'

'But Mrs Darlow, it wasn't exactly my fault. I didn't start it,' I protested.

I wasn't going to tell tales on Justine Scarlet-Fountain-For-A-Nose Littlewood, but I felt I needed to indicate that I'd been Severely Provoked.

Mrs Darlow clapped her hands at me to shut me up. 'In my experience it's *always* your fault, Tracy Beaker,' she said.

This was profoundly unfair. I wished I had enough bottle left to *push punch whack kick* Mrs Darlow. I wanted to see her sprawling on her back, arms and legs flung out, skirts up, knickers showing.

It was such a bizarre image that I couldn't help sniggering. This was fatal.

'How *dare* you act as if this is a laughing matter! I'm tired of your temper tantrums. You're going to have to learn your lesson once and for all. You will not take part in the school play this Christmas!'

'But I have to be in the play, Mrs Darlow. I'm Scrooge. I'm the main part!'

'Not any more,' said Mrs Darlow.

'But my mum's coming to see me!' I said. 'I've written and told her all about it and she's coming specially.'

'I can't help that, Tracy Beaker. You're not taking part in the school play and that's that.'

I lost it then. Totally utterly out-of-it lost it. I opened my mouth and started yelling. Miss Simpkins put her arm round me but I shook her off. Peter clasped my hand but I wrenched it free. I lay down, shut my eyes and shrieked. And shrieked and shrieked and shrieked.

Eventually someone hoicked me up and carted me off to the sickroom. I opened my eyes momentarily. Justine Hate-Her-Guts Littlewood was sitting on a chair with her head back, a big wodge of tissues clutched to her bleeding nose. I closed my eyes and carried on shrieking.

I heard murmurings and mutterings. When I next opened my eyes I couldn't see Justine. I didn't know what had happened to her. I didn't care. I wished everyone in the whole world would disappear. Everyone except my mum.

I thought about Mum getting her Christmas presents, looking at her copy of A Christmas Carol, dressing up in her prettiest clothes and tying her heart necklace round her neck, rubbing her hand lotion on her slim fingers and applying her new lipstick into a shiny pink smile. I saw her arriving at the school on 20 December, sitting right at the front ready to watch me act. Only I wouldn't be in it. I wouldn't be in it. I wouldn't be in it.

I shrieked some more, even though my throat ached and my head thumped and I was burning hot and wet with sweat. I knew it was time to stop howling but I couldn't. I tried clamping my mouth shut but the shrieks built up inside and then came shouting out louder than ever. It was so scary that I started shaking. I couldn't stop. I was cursed like a creature in a fairy tale, condemned to scream for all eternity.

Then I felt new hands on my shoulders and Jenny's familiar firm voice.

'Easy, Tracy. It's OK. I'm here now. They sent for me. Now stop the noise.'

'I . . . can't!' I shrieked.

'Yes, you can. Take deep breaths. In. And now out. That's the ticket. Don't worry, I've got you. You're stopping now, see?'

I clung to Jenny like a little toddler. She knelt down and rocked me while I nuzzled into her shoulder.

'OK now?' she said eventually.

'No!' I paused. I opened my eyes and blinked hard, peering around the room.

'Justine?' I whispered.

75

'She's been taken to hospital,' said Jenny, sighing.

'Oh!'

I started shaking again. What had I *done*? I'd only bopped her on the nose. I'd done that several times before and she'd never been hurt enough to go to *hospital*. What if I'd hit her so hard her entire nose had burst and now she just had a big bloody blob in the middle of her face? What if her whole *head* had exploded and now they were trying to stitch all the bits back together again?

I hated Justine and I always would but I didn't want her to be seriously *hurt*. What if she didn't get better? What if she bled so much she died? I pictured her lying there limp and white in hospital, doctors and nurses and Louise and Justine's dad gathered round her bedside.

I saw her funeral, all the Dumping Ground kids trailing along in black behind her hearse. I saw Louise weeping, carrying a huge wreath.

I tried to tell her I was sorry, but she turned on me and told me I was a murderer. Everyone started murmuring the awful word – *Murderer, murderer, Tracy Beaker is a murderer* – and then I heard sirens and a whole squad of police cars arrived and the police leaped out and ran towards me brandishing their truncheons and I started to run in terror, screaming—

'Tracy! Don't start again,' said Jenny. 'I'm sure Justine is OK. Well, she's not, her poor nose bled horribly and you are going to be severely punished for it, my girl, but I don't think there's any long-term harm. Mrs Darlow is worried you might have broken Justine's nose, but I think she's over-reacting a little. Now, I'm going to take you back home. You need to calm down in the Quiet Room. Then we'll talk things over and see what we can do.'

I let her steer me out of the room and down the corridor. The bell had gone for play time and there were hordes of kids milling up and down, staring staring staring.

'Look at Tracy Beaker!'

'What's the matter with Tracy Beaker?'

'Hey, someone said she's had this ginormous tantrum and screamed her head off.'

'She screamed all sorts of bad words at Mrs Darlow!'

'She attacked Justine Littlewood and she's been rushed to hospital in an ambulance!'

'She punched Mrs Darlow right on the nose!'

'She's not allowed to be in the school play any more!'

I moaned and snorted and sniffled. Jenny gave me a gentle push past them all, out through the doors and across the playground. I started shivering and shaking, knuckling my eyes to try to dry them up.

I hated it that so many of them had seen me in a state. It's different at the Dumping Ground. Everyone understands that looked-after kids are a bit like fireworks with very short fuses. Beware matches! Some of us just do a little fizz and whizz when someone sets them off. Weedy Peter's mini-tantrums are like little kiddy sparklers. Some of us explode loudly like bangers, but it's all over quickly without too much show. And *some* of us are like mega rockets and we soar and swoop and explode into a million stars.No prizes for guessing which firework *I* fit.

They don't get it at school. They especially don't get me. I didn't mind them knowing I'd socked Justine. I rather liked it that they thought I'd punched Mrs Darlow. But I hated them all seeing me in such a state, all blood, sweat and tears. I didn't mind the blood, I didn't mind the sweat, but Tracy Beaker doesn't cry. Ever. Not publicly, anyway.

The minivan was a very private place. And so is the Quiet Room. And my bedroom. Jenny said I could come down to tea but I didn't fancy the idea.

Mike brought a tray upstairs to my room.

'Hey, Tracy. I know you're in disgrace, but I wouldn't want you to miss out on spag bol, and it's particularly tasty tonight.'

He thrust the tray under my nose. My nostrils prickled with the rich savoury smell, but I turned my head away.

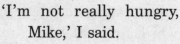

'I'm not really hungry, Mike,' I said.

'Miss Fussy-Gussy. I've slaved at the stove for hours so the least you can do is try a mouthful,' said Mike, balancing the tray on my lap and twisting spaghetti round and round the fork. 'Come on, sweetie. Here's an aeroplane – *wheee* through the air and *in* it swoops,' he said, guying the way he fed the very little kids in the Dumping Ground.

I kept my lips clamped. I didn't even smile at him. I didn't feel in the mood for jokes (even sweet ones) or food (though spag bol was a special favourite).

'Come on, Tracy. Even Justine hasn't lost her appetite, yet she's the girl with the poorly nose.'

'Is she back from the hospital?' I said.

'Yep. Poor, poor Justine,' said Mike.

'Is her nose really broken?' I whispered.

'Broken right *off*,' said Mike – but then he saw my expression. '*Joke*, Tracy. It's fine. You just gave her a little nosebleed. But Jenny and I have got to put our heads together and find some suitable means of punishment. You've got to learn to handle your temper, Tracy, especially at school. Jenny and I are sick of apologizing to old Dragon Darlow. She's always been a tad wary of all our kids – you in particular, Ms Biff and Bash Beaker. Every time you throw a wobbly at school you're confirming all her prejudices.'

'You can punish me any way you want,' I said wanly. 'You can beat me and starve me and lock me in the cupboard.'

'There's not much point,' said Mike. 'If I tried to beat you I'm sure you'd beat me right back. You're already starving yourself going without your spag bol. And there's no point shutting you in the art cupboard because I have a shrewd suspicion you know how to pick that lock already. No, I think we'll have to come up with something more to the point.'

'I told you, Mike, I don't care. Mrs Darlow's punished me already. She won't let me be Scrooge any more and my mum won't get to see me act,' I said.

Some drops of water dribbled down my face and splashed into the plate of spaghetti on my lap.

'I know how tough that is, Tracy,' Mike said, and he gave me a little hug. 'I know how hard you've worked on your part, and I'm sure you'd have been the Scroogiest Scrooge ever. I think we both know that we can't take it for granted that your mum can come to see you – but if she *did* just happen to be there she'd be so proud of you, sweetheart. All the kids think Mrs Darlow's being very unfair. They say the play won't be the same without you, Tracy.'

'Who are you trying to kid, Mike?' I said wearily, but I reached out and tried a very small forkful of spaghetti. It was still hot and surprisingly tasty.

'I mean it, Tracy. Little Peter's absolutely beside himself. He's thinking of starting up some petition.'

'Ah. Sweet,' I said, trying another forkful. 'Still, I bet Louise and

Justine are thrilled to bits that I'm out of the play.'

'Well, you're wrong then, chum. I know you three aren't the best of mates nowadays, but Louise seems quite uncomfortable about the situation. I think she feels she and Justine might just have provoked your sudden savage attack.'

'Really?' I said, starting to scoop up my spag bol enthusiastically. 'What about Justine? What does she say?'

'Well, she's probably the only one of the kids who isn't as yet a signed-up member of the Justice for Tracy Fan Club. That's hardly surprising as her poor nose is still swollen and sore.'

'Oh dear,' I said insincerely.

Mike ruffled my curls. 'You're a bad bad girl, little Beaker. We're going to have to channel all that aggression somehow.' That sounded ominous.

I was right to be suspicious. The next morning Jenny and Mike cornered me as I came downstairs, head held high, determined to show everyone I was absolutely fine now, so long as everyone kept their gob shut about mums and plays and headteachers.

I held my head a little too high, so I couldn't see where I was going. Some stupid little kid had set a small herd of plastic dinosaurs to graze on the carpet at the foot of the stairs. I skidded and very nearly went bonk on my bum again, but this time my natural grace and agility enabled me to keep my footing – just.

'Why don't you make the kids clear up all their little plastic whatsits?' I demanded.

'Good point, Tracy,' said Mike.

'Maybe you'll help us, Tracy,' said Jenny. 'It will make your job easier.'

I paused. I eyed them suspiciously. 'What job?'

'We've thought of an excellent way to channel your aggression,' said Mike.

'Don't think of this as a punishment, Tracy. It's a positive way to make this a happy, clean and tidy home,' said Jenny.

The words *clean* and *tidy* reverberated ominously, scouring my ears.

'Hey, you're not plotting that I'm going to be,

like, your *cleaning lady*?' I said.

'Quick off the mark as always, Tracy Beaker,' said Mike.

'We feel you'll do an excellent job,' said Jenny.

'You can't force me! There's a law against child labour!' I protested.

'We're not employing you, Tracy. We're simply helping you manage your anger in a practical fashion.'

'What sort of practical?'

'You just have to tidy and dust and vacuum and clean the bathrooms and give the kitchen floor a quick scrub.'

I thought quickly. 'So how much are you going to pay me?'

'Ah. Well, we thought you would want to do this first week as a trial run. If you want a permanent position after that I'm sure we could start financial negotiations,' said Jenny. 'Now,

85

run and have your breakfast or you'll be late for school.'

'But—'

'No buts, Tracy,' said Mike firmly.

I know when it's a waste of Beaker breath pursuing a point. I stamped into the kitchen and sat down at the table. I shook cornflakes into a bowl so violently that they sprayed out onto the table. I poured milk so fiercely that it gushed like Niagara Falls and overflowed my bowl.

They were all staring at me warily. Even Justine looked a little anxious. She kept rubbing her nose.

'Are you OK, Tracy?' Peter squeaked.

'Do I *seem* OK?' I snapped, slamming my spoon down.

Peter jumped and the juice in his cup spilled onto the table.

'For heaven's sake, watch what you're doing!' I said, though I'd actually made much more mess myself. 'I'm the poor cleaning lady now. I've got to mop up after all you lot, so watch out, do you hear me?'

'I should think the people right at the end of the road can hear you,' said Louise. 'And don't pick on poor little Peter. He's started up a petition on your behalf: "Please let Tracy Beaker play Scrooge". He's going to get everyone to sign it.'

'Shh, Louise. It's a secret,' said Peter, blushing.

'Yes, like Mrs Darlow is going to be heavily influenced by Peter's pathetic petition,' I said.

Then I saw his little face. Crumple time again. I felt so mean I couldn't bear it, but I couldn't say anything in front of the others. I just gobbled down my breakfast and then cleared off back to my room to collect my school bag and stuff. I listened out for Peter. I caught him scuttling back from the bathroom, toothpaste round his mouth.

'Hey, Peter!' I hissed.

He jumped again, his tongue nervously licking the white foam off his lips.

'Come in my room a second,' I commanded.

Peter caught his breath. He backed into my bedroom obediently and stood with his back against my Vampire Bat poster, his fists clenched, as if he was facing a firing squad.

'It's OK, Peter,' I said. 'I'm not going to beat you up.'

'I'm sorry if I annoyed you with my petition idea. I know it's a bit silly and maybe pointless but I felt so bad about you not being in the play any more and I just wanted to do something.'

'I was just being a bad-tempered pig at breakfast. I didn't mean to get cross with you, Pete. I think your petition's a lovely idea. Nobody's ever put me in a petition before. I still don't see that it will *achieve* anything, but I think it's ever so sweet of you. You're a very special friend. Thank you. Ever so much.'

Peter still didn't move but he went raspberry-red and blinked at me rapidly.

'Oh, Tracy,' he said.

I gave him a little pat on the head. He tried to

give me a big hug but I wasn't prepared to go *that* far.

'Hey, watch out, you're wiping toothpaste all over me. Come on, we'll be late for school.'

'So can I carry on with my petition?'

'Feel free. Though I doubt you'll get many people to sign it on account of the fact that I'm not the most popular girl in the school. Um . . . have the kids here *really* signed it?'

'Yes, all of them. Well, Justine hasn't quite managed to get round to it yet, but I'll keep badgering her.'

'Oh, Peter, you couldn't badger anyone!'

'You wait and see, Tracy. I'll get the whole school to sign the petition. You *have* to be in the play. You're totally brilliant at acting Scrooge.'

'You're wasting your time, Pete, but thanks anyway,' I said. 'It's great that you've got such faith in my acting abilities. Tell you what, when I'm grown up and a famous movie star just like my mum, I'll let you be my agent, OK?'

This perked him up no end but it had the opposite effect on me. Just mentioning my mum made me want to start howling again. But I had to go to school and control all emotion. Yesterday I'd screamed and shrieked. Today I was going to be calm and in control to show everyone that Tracy Beaker is One Tough Cookie, able to cope with incredible public humiliation without turning a hair.

It wasn't as easy as that. I jumped out of the Dumping Ground minivan and walked into school as nonchalantly as possible, but everyone in the playground turned and stared and pointed at me. A group of little kids actually stood round me in a circle as if they could turn me on like a television and watch *The Tracy Beaker Freak Show*.

The kids staring at me wasn't the worse part. It was the teachers. They were crazily *kind* to me. Miss Brown actually hovered by my desk when she was collecting up maths homework and said softly, 'How are you doing, Tracy?'

Miss Brown

'Not too good, Miss Brown,' I muttered.

'I don't suppose you managed to do your maths homework last night?'

'I was kind of Otherwise Engaged,' I said.

'Oh well. Not to worry. You can do it in your lunch hour.'

'OK, I've got all the time in the world in my lunch hour now,' I said, sighing heavily.

The lunch hour was dreadful. Peter and Louise and Justine and all the other kids in *A Christmas Carol* rushed off to the hall to rehearse . . . without me.

I stayed in the classroom all by myself and did my maths homework. The inky numbers on my page kept blurring and blotching, as if they were being rained on. I used up two tissues and my sleeve mopping up.

I whizzed along to the cloakroom just before

the start of afternoon school to splash cold water on my face – and bumped into Miss Simpkins. She had Gloria Taylor, Emily Lawson and Amy Jellicoe with her. They were all looking up at her hopefully, eyes huge like puppies in Battersea Dogs Home, going, *Pick me, Miss Simpkins*.

'Oh, Tracy,' said Miss Simpkins. She waved her hand at Gloria and Emily and Amy. 'Run along, girls. I'll let you know tomorrow,' she said.

They each gave me a pitying glance and then ran off obediently.

'They've been auditioning for Scrooge, haven't they?' I said flatly.

'Yes, they have,' said Miss Simpkins. She lowered her voice to a whisper. 'And they all tried their best, but strictly between you and me, Tracy, they're rubbish compared to you.'

'So which one are you going to pick, Miss Simpkins?'

'I don't know,' she said, sighing. 'It's such a

big part and there's hardly any time left to learn it. Gloria's the only girl who could learn it all by heart, but she runs through it like a railway station announcer, with no expression whatsoever. Emily can at least act a little, but she can't remember two consecutive lines so she'd have to have the script in her hands the whole time and that would spoil things.'

'So are you going to choose Amy for Scrooge?'

'Amy is so sweet and soft and shy she can barely make herself heard and she can't act bad-tempered to save her life. She just doesn't *convince* as Scrooge.'

'Whereas I can act bad-tempered till the cows come home,' I said.

'Yes! You were my magnificent Scrooge,' she said, sighing.

'Until Mrs Darlow spoiled everything,' I said.

'No, Tracy. Until *you* spoiled everything,' said Miss Simpkins. 'Although I know you were severely provoked. I've tried explaining the circumstances to Mrs Darlow – in vain, I'm sorry to say.'

'Well. Thank you, Miss Simpkins,' I said. 'I'm sorry I mucked it all up.'

'It seems a shame you've got to pay so dearly

for it,' said Miss Simpkins.

'You don't know the half of it,' I said darkly. 'I'm paying for it with knobs on, even back at the Home. I'm acting as an unpaid skivvy clearing up after all the kids. Isn't that unbelievably unfair? I think you should report them to the NSPCC, OK?'

'I'll think about it,' said Miss Simpkins, but she was struggling hard not to laugh.

I *certainly* didn't feel like laughing when I came home utterly exhausted from school to have Jenny hand me the hoover and Mike thrust the mop and bucket at me.

I'd been secretly hoping that this was one big bluff. I was outraged to realize they really meant to go through with it.

'Let me have my tea first, for pity's sake,' I said.

I took my time munching my banana wholemeal sandwich and my handful of nuts and my orange and my apple juice. (Oh for the days of unhealthy eating when we wolfed down crisps and chocolate and cakes and Coke.) Then I stomped off to my room to change out of my school uniform and put on my oldest jeans and faded T-shirt.

I stopped to look at the postcard from Mum on my notice board. I suddenly felt so sad I had to lie on my bed with my head under my pillow just in case anyone overheard my sudden attack of hay fever. I was still feeling sniffly when I trailed down the stairs, sighing considerably. No one was around to hear me. The other kids all seemed to be whispering together in the kitchen. It was all right for *some* Ugly People. Poor little Cinderella Beaker had to stay home and tackle all the chores.

I picked up the hoover, switched it on and started shoving it backwards and forwards across the hall. It was so heavy, so clumsy, so awkward. My arms were aching and my back hurt from bending over already and yet I'd only done one weeny patch of carpet. I had the whole huge Dumping Ground to render spotless. I banged the hoover violently into the skirting board and gave it a kick. I was only wearing soft shoes. It hurt *horribly*. I switched the hateful hoover off and doubled up, nursing my poor stubbed toes.

I heard more whisperings and gigglings.

'Shut up, you lot!' I snarled.

Peter popped his head round the kitchen door. 'Tracy, are you *OK*?'

'I'm absolutely in the pink,' I said sarcastically. 'In the rose-pink, salmon-pink, petunia-pink – *not*. How do you think I feel, knowing I've got the tremendous task of cleaning up the Dumping Ground single-handed?'

'Not *quite* single-handed,' said Peter. 'Come on, gang!'

All the kids suddenly sprang out of the kitchen into the hall. Peter stood in front, jersey sleeves rolled up his puny little arms, a tea towel tied round his waist like a pinny. They were all clutching dusters and mops and brushes and pans. Louise was there, her long hair tied up in a scarf. Justine sloped out last, wearing Mike's stripy cooking apron and wielding a scrubbing brush.

'We're all going to do the cleaning,' said Peter.
'It seemed so horribly mean that you had to do
it all, so we're helping out. It'll be fun!'

'Not *my* idea of fun, you little runt,' said
Justine, juggling her scrubbing brush.

Louise caught it and held onto it. 'It was just as much our fault as yours, Tracy,' she said. 'We *all* got mad, so Peter's right, we should all channel our aggression into housework.'

'So OK, troops, let's get cracking!' Peter said. He looked at me. 'OK, Tracy?'

For once I was totally speechless. I just nodded very hard and blinked very hard and hoped very hard that I wouldn't utterly disgrace myself and howl. We let funny little Peter order us around, telling each of us what to do, because it was easier than us big ones arguing about it. We put radios playing the loudest rock and rap music in every corner of the Dumping Ground and then set to with a vengeance.

Elaine the Pain came calling halfway through. She cowered backwards, covering her ears, but when Jenny and Mike explained (having to bellow a bit), she clapped her hands excitedly and went prancing around congratulating everyone on their team spirit.

'It reflects the very essence of Christmas, loving and sharing and caring,' she said, jamming her reindeer antlers on her head and rushing around giving everyone a little pat on the back.

It's a wonder Elaine Ridiculous Reindeer Pain didn't make them think: *What on earth am I doing scrubbing away when I could be watching the telly or playing on my Xbox or simply lounging on my bed picking my nose because I definitely don't love Tracy Beaker and I don't care tuppence about her and I certainly don't want to share her stupid punishment*. But somehow they took no notice and carried on dusting and scrubbing and scouring and hoovering. I felt as if all the dirty grubby grimy greasy little bits of me were getting a clean and polish too. Maybe they did like me just a little bit after all.

I still had some stuff left over from my raid on the art cupboard. That night I laboured long and hard over a big card. I drew the Dumping Ground and all of us guys outside, armed with dusters and brushes and mops. I even drew Justine properly, though it was very tempting to cross her eyes and scribble little bogeys hanging from her nose. I put me in the centre with a big beaming smile. I drew little rays of sunshine all round my picture and then I printed at the top in dead artistic rainbow lettering:

I crept downstairs and stuck it on the table so that everyone would see it at breakfast time. I snaffled half a packet of cornflakes and an orange so I could have breakfast in my room. I didn't want to be hanging around when they saw the card. It would be *way* too embarrassing. I wasn't used to acting all mushy and saying thank you. I'd have to watch it. I was used to being the toughest kid on the block. It would be fatal to soften up now.

I tried hard to be my normal fierce and feisty self at school. I summoned up all my energy to cheek the teachers and argue with the kids but it was hard work. I found myself sharing my chocolate bar with Peter in the playground and picking up some little kid who'd fallen over and kicking someone's ball straight back to them, acting like Ms Goody-Goody Two Trainers instead of the Tough and Terrible Tracy Beaker,

When everyone went to rehearse *A Christmas Carol* I wondered which of the Three Stooges Miss Simpkins had picked as Scrooge. I couldn't help being glad that they were all pretty useless.

Halfway through the first lesson in the afternoon Mrs Darlow sent for me.

'Oh, Tracy,' said Miss Brown sorrowfully. 'What have you been up to *now*?'

'Nothing, Miss Brown!' I said. 'I've been a positive angel all day.'

Miss Brown didn't look as if she believed me. I couldn't really blame her. She wasn't to know I was this new squeaky-clean sweet-as-honey Beaker.

I plodded along to Mrs Darlow's study, wondering if she was going to blame me for someone else's misdemeanour. Maybe she'd think *I'd* written the very very rude rhyme in the girls' toilets. Maybe she'd think *I'd* superglued some teacher's chair. Maybe she'd think *I'd* climbed up the drainpipe after a lost ball and pulled the pipe right off the wall in the process. I *had* done all these things in the past, but not *recently*.

Still, I would doubtless be blamed. I sighed wearily and knocked on Mrs Darlow's door, deciding that there was no point protesting my total innocence to such a grim and unforgiving woman. She was doubtless preparing to Punish Tracy Beaker Severely. I saw her selecting her whippiest whip, her thumb crunchers, her nose tweakers, clearing her desk of superfluous paperwork so she could stretch me across it as if I was on a torture rack. I'd crawl out of school lashed into bloody stripes, thumbs mangled, nose pulled past my chin, stretched out and out and out like elastic.

Mrs Darlow was wearing her severest black trouser suit. She sat at her desk, her chin in her hands, frowning at me over the top of her glasses.

'Come and sit down, Tracy Beaker,' she said.

She always says my name in full, though there isn't another Tracy in the whole school.

'How are you today?' she enquired.

'Not especially happy, Mrs Darlow,' I said.

'Neither am I, Tracy Beaker, neither am I,' she said. She took hold of a large wad of paper scribbled all over with lots of names. 'Do you know what this is?'

I paused. I had a feeling that it wasn't the time to say 'pieces of paper'.

'I don't know, Mrs Darlow' seemed a safer bet. I truly didn't know. The handwriting wasn't mine. It was all different writing, some neat, some scrawly, in black, blue, red – all the colours of the rainbow.

'This is a petition to reinstate you as Scrooge in the school play,' said Mrs Darlow.

'Oh goodness! Peter's petition!' I said.

'Are you sure you didn't put him up to it, Tracy Beaker?'

'Absolutely not!' I said. 'But he's got heaps and heaps of signatures!'

'Yes, he has. Though I've scrutinized every page, and some of the signatures are duplicated – and I'm not sure Mickey Mouse, Homer Simpson, Robbie Williams and Beyoncé are actually pupils at this school.'

My mouth twitched. I was scared I was going to get the giggles, and yet my eyes were pricking as if I had a bout of hay fever coming on. All those signatures! I thought of Peter going round and round and round the whole school with his petition and all those kids signing away, wanting *me* in the play.

'Peter's obviously a very kind friend,' said Mrs Darlow.

'Yes, he is,' I said humbly.

'I'm rather impressed by his initiative and perseverance. When he delivered the petition this morning he was trembling all over, but he still made his own personal impassioned plea. He stated – accurately – that there is no other girl remotely like you, Tracy Beaker.'

I smiled.

'He meant it as a compliment. I didn't,' said Mrs Darlow. 'I felt very sorry for poor Peter when I told him that it was highly unlikely I would change my mind, even though I was very impressed by his petition.'

'Oh,' I said, slumping in my chair.

'Then I had a visit from Miss Simpkins at lunch time. She's already tried to plead your cause, Tracy Beaker. She's told me that your appalling assault wasn't entirely unprovoked. However, I've explained to her that I can never condone violent behaviour, no matter what the circumstances.'

I sighed and slumped further down the chair.

'However . . .' said Mrs Darlow.

I stiffened.

'Miss Simpkins invited me along to rehearsals. The play itself is progressing perfectly. Everyone's worked very hard.

I watched Gloria and Emily and Amy play Scrooge, one after the other. They tried extremely hard. In fact I awarded them five team points each for endeavour. Unfortunately though, none of the girls is a born actress, and although they tried their best I could see that their performances were a little . . . lacking.'

I clenched my fists.

'Miss Simpkins stressed that *your* performance as Scrooge was extraordinary, Tracy Beaker. I am very aware that this is a *public* performance in front of all the parents.'

'My mum's coming,' I whispered.

'It is a showcase event, and therefore I want everything to be perfect. I don't want all that hard work and effort to be wasted. I've decided to reinstate you, Tracy Beaker. You may play Scrooge after all.'

'Oh, Mrs Darlow! You are a total *angel*!' I said, sitting bolt upright and clapping my hands.

'I'm not sure you're going to

think me so totally angelic by the time I've finished, Tracy Beaker. I said violent behaviour can never be condoned. You must still be severely punished in some other way.'

'*Any* way, Mrs Darlow. Be as inventive as you like. Whips, thumbscrews, nose tweakers, the rack. Whatever.'

'I think I'll select a more mundane punishment, Tracy Beaker, though the nose tweaker sounds tempting,' said Mrs Darlow. 'And appropriate in the circumstances, as you hit poor Justine on *her* nose. However, I'm not sure the school's petty cash can quite cover an instrument of torture. We are already well stocked with cleaning implements so we will stick with those.'

'Cleaning implements, Mrs Darlow?' I said. 'Oh no! I've already had to clean the entire Dumping Ground – I mean, the Home. You're not asking me to clean the whole *school*?'

'As if I'd ask you to do that!' said Mrs Darlow. 'I might not be angelic, but I am reasonable. I think I shall just ask you to clean the hall floor. If we're having all these guests then we can't have the setting looking downright scruffy. I'd like you to stay after school for half an hour every evening and polish up the parquet. It will not only enhance the look of the school, it will also act as a channel for your aggression.'

'My aggression's already been thoroughly channelled, Mrs Darlow,' I said. 'But all right, I will. I'll polish the whole hall until we can all see straight up our skirts, just so long as my mum will be able to see me act Scrooge.'

I don't know if you've ever done any serious polishing? Your hand hurts, your arms ache, your neck twinges, your back's all bent, your knees get rubbed raw, even your toes get scrunched up and sore. Think of the size of a school hall. Think of me.

Long long long did I labour. Dear old Peter and some of the other kids tried to sneak into the hall to help me out, but Mrs Darlow didn't appreciate this kind of caring and sharing teamwork.

'It's Tracy Beaker's punishment, not yours. I want her to labour on her own!' she said.

So labour I did, but I kept a copy of the play in front of me as I polished. I went over and over my lines in my head.

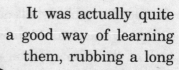

It was actually quite a good way of learning them, rubbing a long line of shiny wood while muttering a long line of Scrooge-speak.

Every time I dipped my cloth into the polish I went, 'Bah! Humbug!' Whenever I finished a whole section I said Tiny Tim's 'God bless us, every one.' By the time I'd polished the entire hall floor I not only knew my lines, I knew everyone else's too.

I couldn't *wait* till Wednesday, the day of our performance. I was in a fever of impatience, positively burning up all over, so much so that Jenny caught hold of me at breakfast and felt my forehead.

'Are you feeling OK, Tracy? You're very flushed.'

'Oh, Tracy, you're not ill, are you?' said Peter. He shivered. '*I* feel ill. I hardly slept last night and when I did I kept dreaming I was standing on the stage all alone and people kept shouting rude things to me. I wish wish wish I didn't have

110

to act. I'm simply dreading tonight. What if I forget what to say?'

'You'll be fine, Pete. You won't forget. And if you *do*, just look at me and I'll whisper them for you,' I said.

'Yeah, the one and only Big-mouth Beaker,' sneered Justine.

She didn't look too well herself. She was very pale, with dark circles under her eyes.

'You look like Marley's Ghost already, without bothering with make-up,' I said. 'Getting worried you'll be rubbish?'

'Absolutely *not*.' Justine paused. 'What about you, Tracy? Are you getting worried? Worried your mum might not turn up to watch you? Ha, that's a laugh. Your mum's as rarely sighted as the Abominable Snowman.'

There was a sudden silence. Everyone stopped chomping their cornflakes.

'Justine, button that lip!' said Mike.

'Tracy, don't start anything!' said Jenny.

I wasn't going to show Justine Spooky-Spectre Littlewood she could rattle me. I smiled at her, teeth clenched. I felt my tummy clenching too, into a tight little ball. Mum *would* come, wouldn't she?

She'd surely want to see me act the leading part in our school play. She'd want to sit right in the middle, surrounded by happy clapping parents, all of them saying, 'That Tracy Beaker's a great little actress. I wonder where she gets that from?' Then they'd look round and spot Mum, all glamorous and gorgeous, and go, '*She* must be Tracy's mum. Oh my goodness, of *course*! She's the movie star Carly Beaker!'

She'd be there tonight, clutching her copy of *A Christmas Carol*, wearing her lipstick and her hand cream and her heart necklace. She'd *have* to come when I'd tried so hard with her presents. She'd want to give me a big hug and kiss and clap till her hands smarted, and then she'd sweep me off for ever because she was so proud of me.

'Dream on, Tracy,' Justine Poison-Mouth Littlewood muttered.

The fist inside my tummy squeezed tighter. *Was* it all a daydream? Was I really just kidding myself?

'My mum *is* coming, just you wait and see,' I said.

'I'll be waiting – and we'll all be seeing,' said Justine About-To-Get-Her-Nose-Punched-Again Littlewood. 'We'll see my dad sitting there clapping away, but whoops, there'll be this *empty* seat right in the middle of the row where Mother Beaker's bottom should be, only she can't be bothered to come and see her only daughter – and who can blame her when she's as bonkers and batty and totally bananas as Tracy Beaker—'

I leaped up but Jenny caught hold of me and Mike hustled Justine out of the room.

'Cool it, Tracy,' said Jenny.

I couldn't cool it. I was burning up, about to erupt like a volcano. But then Peter clutched my hand.

'Take no notice of Justine. She's just jealous because you're such a brilliant actress and everyone signed my petition because they all know the play wouldn't work without you. And if you say your mum's coming, then of course she will. You always know everything, Tracy.'

I took a deep deep deep breath and then squeezed his hand.

'That's right, Peter,' I said. 'Thanks, pal. Don't fret. I wouldn't let a sad twisted girl like Justine wind me up.'

Jenny gave me a quick hug. 'Well done, girl.'

'Jenny?' I took another even deeper deeper deeper breath. 'I *know* my mum's coming, and I sent her all the details and all this stuff, but I don't suppose she's been on the phone just to *confirm* she's coming?'

'You know I'd have told you, Tracy.'

'Yeah, yeah, well . . . As if she *needs* to tell us. I mean, we can just take it as read, can't we?' I said.

'I'm coming,' said Jenny. 'And Mike. We're getting extra help here just so we can watch you. Elaine's coming. Don't pull that face, Tracy! Cam's coming. It will be wonderful if your mum comes too, but you'll still have lots of people in the audience absolutely rooting for you. OK?'

It wasn't OK at all. This was Careworker

115

Evasive-Speak. I *couldn't* take it as read that my mum was coming.

I knew that.

I didn't *want* to know.

I tried very very very hard indeed to take it as read. It was as if it was printed everywhere and I was literally reading it over and over again. I stared round the kitchen and saw it spelled out in spaghetti shapes all round the walls.

YOUR MUM'S COMING TO SEE YOU ACT SCROOGE

I went to the toilet and I saw it scribbled all over the door.

Your Mum's coming to see you act Scrooge.

I went to school in the minivan and I saw it flash up on the dashboard.

YOUR MUM'S COMING TO SEE YOU ACT SCROOGE

I looked out of the window and saw it on all the posters in town.

YOUR MUM'S COMING TO SEE YOU ACT SCROOGE

I got to school and it was chalked on the blackboard.

Your Mum's coming to see you act Scrooge.

I stood in assembly and it shone above the stage.

YOUR MUM'S COMING TO SEE YOU ACT SCROOGE.

The words flashed on and off in my mind all day long like little fairy lights.

YOUR MUM'S COMING TO SEE YOU ACT SCROOGE.

I couldn't concentrate on a thing in class. I thought Henry the Sixth had eight wives, I couldn't even do short division, let alone long, I ran the wrong way in the obstacle race in PE, I coloured Santa's beard scarlet on my Christmas card. Luckily Miss Brown just laughed at me.

'I know you've got other things on your mind today, Tracy. Good luck with the play tonight. I'm so looking forward to it.'

But I *didn't* have the play on my mind. I couldn't get it *in* my mind. We had a last rehearsal

117

at lunch time, gabbling through our lines one last time. I stumbled and stuttered and couldn't remember a thing.

'I don't know what's gone wrong, Miss Simpkins!' I said frantically. 'I'm word perfect, I know I am. I could chant the whole play backwards yesterday, I swear I could.'

'I knew Tracy Beaker would mess up royally,' Justine whispered to Louise, though it was a loud enough whisper for me to hear.

'It's simply last-minute nerves, Tracy,' said Miss Simpkins. 'You'll be fine tonight. Don't worry about it.'

She was doing her best to be reassuring – but *she* looked worried. I could see her thinking, *Oh my Lord, I've gone out on a limb to keep problem kid Tracy in the play and now she can't even say a simple line! What have I done? I must keep smiling, stay calm. I'm not going to panic. I'll just tell the kid she'll be fine tonight.*

For the first and only time in my life I was in

total agreement with Justine Smug-Slug Littlewood. It looked like I was going to mess up royally.

We didn't go home for our tea. All the children in the cast had a packed picnic on my wondrously polished hall floor. If I'd been my usual self I'd have been incensed. They were spilling sandwich crumbs and scattering crisps all over the place. One of the kids even poured a carton of sticky squash all over my floor! But I was in such a state I barely noticed. I couldn't even eat my picnic. My egg sandwich tasted of old damp flannel, my crisps stuck in my throat, my yoghurt smelled sour.

'Eat up, Tracy. You're going to be burning up a lot of energy tonight,' said Peter. 'Here, do you want half my special banana sandwich? Hey, you can have all of it if you like.'

'Thanks, Pete – but no thanks,' I said.

I sat and brooded, snapping all my crisps into tiny golden splinters. I didn't know what to do.

I so so so wanted my mum to come and see me, but did I really want her to see me standing sweating on stage, mouth open, but no words whatsoever coming out?

I shut my eyes tight. 'Please, if there really is a Spirit of Christmas Past, a Spirit of Christmas Present and a Spirit of Christmas Yet to Come, help me now, and then I'll out-do Tiny Tim with my "God bless you"s,' I said inside my head.

I sensed someone standing beside me. I opened my eyes, hoping desperately that it might be Mum, with her lovely long golden curls, her big blue eyes, her glossy pink lips all ready to kiss me . . . but I was staring at this small scruffy woman with short sticking-up hair.

'Oh, it's only you, Cam,' I said wearily.

'Happy Christmas to you too, Tracy,' said Cam, laughing.

'What are you doing here? The play's not for hours yet.'

'I know. I've come to help your Miss Simpkins do your make-up.'

120

'But you don't know anything about it! You never *wear* make-up.'

'I'm great at stage make-up, you wait and see.'

She sat down cross-legged beside me. She was wearing her usual jeans and jersey – but they were her newest not-frayed-at-the-hems jeans and she was wearing her best jumper with the knitted cats.

She thrust a big box of chocolates at me.

'Here. Have a nibble, then pass them round to all your pals.'

'Oh, Cam. Did you buy them specially for me?'

'Well, not exactly,' said Cam. 'They were going to be for my mum, when I went home for Christmas. Only I'm not actually *going* home as it turns out, so I thought we could have them now.'

'Well, it's very kind of you but I'm not a bit hungry. I feel kind of sick. Maybe I'm going to throw up on stage. If I do I hope it's when Justine's doing her Marley's Ghost bit,' I said.

I opened the box of chocolates all the same, simply out of curiosity. They were extra-special wonderful chocs, all sleek and shiny, some

121

wrapped in pink and silver and gold paper, others dotted with cherries and nuts and little crystallized roses.

'Oh, yum,' I said automatically. My fingers reached out for the biggest cherry chocolate of their own accord. I gave it one little lick and then popped it in my mouth quick.

I chewed, and the most beautiful cherry chocolate taste oozed all over my tongue and round my teeth.

'Mmm!' I said. My hand reached out again.

'I wouldn't have too many if you're feeling sick,' said Cam.

'Do you know something weird? I'm starting to feel just a tiny bit better. Hey, these are seriously scrumptious chocolates. Do I really have to hand them round? I'll have just *one* more, OK? Your mum's really missing out big-time. Why aren't you going to see her at Christmas then?'

'Oh. We had a row. We always have rows. I phoned her to ask if I could bring someone with me.'

'Who? Not a boyfriend!'

'I've *told* you, Tracy, I haven't got a boyfriend. This was someone else, but anyway, she didn't like that idea, and then she went on about this party she's giving, and saying stuff like will I please have my hair done and could I wear a decent skirt and proper heels.' Cam sighed. 'She's impossible.'

'No, she's not. You'd look *heaps* better with your hair done all fancy and a nice tight skirt, and why on earth *don't* you wear heels? My mum always does.'

I shouldn't have said the word *mum*. My tummy went tight all over again. I was on my fourth chocolate by this time. It didn't seem such a great idea.

Cam held my hand. 'Your mum's obviously a glamorous girly mum. I'm more your *casual* woman. Though *my* mum would say there's casual and there's downright ragbag.'

'Oh, Cam, do *you* think my mum will come to see me act Scrooge?'

Cam gripped my hand tightly. 'I'm sure she *wants* to come, badly. It's just . . . she could be tied up somewhere.'

'I'm going to let her down if she *does* come.' I crept closer to Cam. I hissed in her ear so none of the other kids could hear. 'I was totally rubbish at the rehearsal at lunch time. I couldn't remember a single word.'

'That's great, Tracy,' said Cam brightly.

'That's *great*?' I said. 'Oh thanks, Cam! I thought you were supposed to be my *friend*? It's great that Tracy Beaker is going to publicly humiliate herself in front of the whole school, all the parents, everyone from the Dumping Ground and her own *mother*?'

'I *am* your friend and I'm talking sense. Everyone knows that it's bad luck to have a dress rehearsal that goes really well. The worse it is, the better the actual performance.'

'You're kidding!'

'No, no, it's common knowledge in the acting profession. I'm surprised your mum hasn't told you. So you'll be great tonight, Tracy, you'll see.'

'But I can't remember a single line! What am I meant to do? *Mime* it all?'

'Well, I'm sure you'd mime very expressively, but I don't think that will be necessary. The moment you get on stage I'm sure you'll be word perfect again. The lines are all in there, Tracy.'

She swung our clasped hands upwards and gently tapped my head. 'You just need to press the right button and they'll come bursting out as easily as anything, believe me.'

I looked at her. I *didn't* believe her – but I was touched that she was trying so hard to convince me. I looked at Cam's best outfit. I looked at her earnest face and her funny scrubbing-brush haircut. I suddenly gave her a big hug right there in front of everyone.

Some skinny little kid playing Ignorance in the play piped up, 'Is that your mum, Tracy?'

'She's not my *real* mum,' I said. 'But she's kind of *like* a mum to me.'

Cam gave me a big hug back. 'That's the nicest thing you've ever said about me, Tracy,' she said.

'It's all this Christmas Peace and Goodwill stuff. It's getting to me,' I said.

I passed all the chocolates round. I *even* offered one to Justine, which was a waste of time.

'You've probably gobbed all over them, Tracy Beaker,' she said.

Mrs Darlow came trit-trotting out of her office,

in through the swing doors and over my beautifully shiny floor to wish us all luck.

Miss Simpkins came scurrying to my side, looking tense. I smiled at her reassuringly and offered Mrs Darlow a chocolate.

'Good luck, Tracy Beaker,' she said, popping a nut cluster in her mouth.

'Mind how you go in those little heels, Mrs Darlow. We don't want you slipping on the highly polished floor,' I said politely.

'Ah, yes. You've worked hard, Tracy. It's a little patchy here and there, but on the whole you've done a splendid job. Nothing beats a bit of elbow grease. I'm almost tempted to do away with the electric polisher and employ you on a permanent basis.'

'You have an electric polisher?' I said faintly. 'Yet you let me polish the entire floor by *hand*?'

'Tracy!' Cam hissed.

I took a deep breath. 'So the hall floor *could* have been polished in a matter of minutes, Mrs Darlow?'

'But that wouldn't have been such an excellent . . . what was the phrase? A channel for your aggression!' said Mrs Darlow, smiling at me. Triumphantly.

I looked at her. She looked at me. Cam was on one side of me, Miss Simpkins on the other. I knew both were holding their breath.

I suddenly burst out laughing. 'Nice one, Mrs Darlow,' I said. 'You win.'

'Thank you,' said Mrs Darlow. 'So you win tonight, Tracy Beaker. Act your little socks off.'

She zigzagged her way through the picnicking cast as if she was performing a complicated country dance and went out of the hall.

Cam and Miss Simpkins blew out their cheeks and sighed 'Pheeeeeew' simultaneously.

'You both thought I was going to blow it, didn't you?' I said.

'Well, the thought did just cross my mind,' said Miss Simpkins.

'It crossed and recrossed and danced up and down in *my* mind,' said Cam. She scrabbled in the chocolate box, found another great big cherry

cream and popped it in my mouth. 'Here, kiddo, you deserve it.'

'Now, I suppose we'd better start getting the show on the road,' said Miss Simpkins. 'OK, kids, clear up your picnic stuff as quick as you can. I want all the stagehands to go up on the stage and start sorting out the backdrops. I'll come and help in a minute. All the rest of you, come and find your costumes. Then, once you're dressed, go to Cam to get made up,' said Miss Simpkins.

'I wish we had *proper* costumes,' Justine complained.

'I do too, Justine, but we haven't had the time, money or indeed expertise to assemble proper Victorian costumes for a large cast. We've done our best with limited resources,' Miss Simpkins said crisply.

We all had to wear our ordinary school uniform, with coats on for everyone playing men. We had cardboard top hats and cardboard bonnets tied with ribbon. The children carol singers simply wound woolly scarves around their necks.

Carol Singer

Victorian Gentleman

Victorian Lady

Marley's Ghost

Miss Simpkins did her best to be inventive with the ghost costumes. Justine as Marley's Ghost had a big bandage round her head and a long dog chain with keys and purses and cash-boxes attached to it with Scoubidou strings.

As the Spirit of Christmas Past, Louise had a white frock and a white veil and her hair brushed out loose past her

Spirit of Christmas Past

shoulders. She danced round and round, pointing her toes.

'I'm glad I've got a pretty costume,' she said.

The Spirit of Christmas Present wore a Santa hat with a white cotton-wool beard and he had sprigs of holly pinned all over him. You couldn't get too near or he'd prick you.

The Spirit of Christmas Yet to Come wore a long black velvet gown (actually Miss Simpkins's dressing gown!) with a black scarf over his head.

Spirit of Christmas Present

Spirit of Christmas Yet to Come

Tiny Tim

That just left Peter and me. He didn't have a special costume as Tiny Tim, just a little cap and a crutch made out of an old broom handle.

I had *two* costumes. I wore my school shirt and grey trousers and an old grey raincoat cut at the back to make proper tails. I also had a white nightshirt with a white cap and slippers with pompoms for my night-time scenes.

Everyone laughed when I tried on the nightshirt, and started spreading rumours that it was *Mrs Darlow's* nightie. I started capering around doing a rude imitation of Mrs Darlow, sticking my bum right out and waggling it. Everyone laughed and I laughed too – though inside I felt so wound up I felt more like crying.

Was my mum going to come???

And if she did, would I let her down?

My capers got wilder. Cam collared me by the scruff of the nightshirt.

'Hey, hey, how about saving the acting for when you go on stage? Get into your Scrooge day outfit and then come to Classroom One. I'll do your make-up first, OK?'

'I don't want any experimenting! You're a total novice when it comes to make-up, Cam.'

'I tell you, I'm a dab hand at stage make-up, trust me. Come on, kiddo. You need to simmer down a little. There's no point being diplomatic with Mrs Darlow one minute and then sending her up rotten the next. If she walked in on your impersonation you'd be toast, Ms Beaker.'

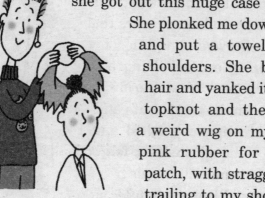

We went to Classroom One together and she got out this huge case of make-up. She plonked me down on a chair and put a towel round my shoulders. She brushed my hair and yanked it into a tight topknot and then crammed a weird wig on my head, half pink rubber for a big bald patch, with straggly grey bits trailing to my shoulders.

'Now for your Scrooge face,' she said, starting to rub pale panstick into my skin.

'Hey, careful! You're getting it in my eyes!'

'Well close them, silly. Come on, Tracy, you want to look the part, don't you? Stop squirming round and act sensible.'

I sat still as a statue, eyes closed, while Cam dabbed and smeared at my face and then stuck stuff all over my eyebrows. She breathed heavily with concentration, tutting if I so much as twitched. Then she patted me lightly under the chin.

'There, Scrooge! You're done.'

I opened my eyes. Cam was holding a mirror in front of me. A mean whey-faced old man with whiskery eyebrows and grey frown lines peered back at me. I gasped – and the old man's thin lips gasped too.

It was me! I could hardly believe it I looked so different.

'I don't look like me any more!'

'Of course you don't. You're *not* you. You're Ebenezer Scrooge, the meanest man in the city.'

'I look *exactly* like the picture in the book I sent my mum . . .' My voice tailed away.

Cam put her face close to mine, her brown eyes big and pleading.

'Tracy. Listen to me. You know sometimes your mum hasn't been able to come to see you because she's making a movie somewhere? Well, that's because she knows how important it is to concentrate on her part. That's what you've got to do now. You're not Tracy Beaker any more, desperate to see her mum. You're Scrooge, and you haven't *got* a mum or a dad or anyone at all. You're a mean old misery-guts who hates everyone, and you especially hate this time of year, Christmas, the season of goodwill, because you don't wish anyone well and you think Christmas is total humbug. Think yourself into the character, Tracy. Don't go and mess around with the others. Stay centred on what you're doing.'

'Bah!' I said. 'Out of my way, Missy. Let me get back to my counting house. I need to give that varmint clerk of mine, Bob Cratchit, a severe talking to.'

Cam grinned and bobbed her head at me. 'Beg pardon, I'm sure, Mr Scrooge,' she said.

So I sloped off into Classroom Two and paced up and down the room telling myself I was Scrooge Scrooge Scrooge. Peter popped his head round the door and asked if I was OK.

'Bah! Humbug!' I growled.

He jumped back, looking upset. 'Sorry, Tracy!'

'I'm not Tracy, I'm Scrooge, you ignorant little lad. When I've been visited by Old Marley and the three Christmas Ghosts I shall have a change of heart and look on you kindly, almost as my own son, but for the moment, hop it!'

Peter hopped it. Literally, using his crutch.

I was fine all the time I was by myself. I thought myself into being Scrooge and acted some of the scenes, bending over like a gnarled old man. But then Miss Simpkins came to find me.

'Ah, Tracy, Cam said you were in here. You make an utterly splendid Scrooge – quite scary! OK, sweetheart, fifteen minutes to go till curtain up. Better whizz to the toilet and then come backstage with all the others.'

Suddenly I got so so so scared I stopped being

135

Scrooge. I didn't even feel like Tracy Beaker any more. I felt like this tiny trembly mini-mouse. My voice turned into a squeak. I had to fight not to hang onto Miss Simpkins's hand like some silly little kid in the Infants. I wanted Cam but she was still making people up in Classroom One.

I had to go and join Justine Hate-Her-Guts Littlewood and Louise and Peter and all the others. They were supposed to be sitting cross-legged at the back of the stage, only speaking in whispers. Of course they were all over the place, giggling and gossiping, clowning around in their costumes. The red velvet stage curtains were pulled shut but Justine ran up to them and had a little peep out.

'I can see him! There's my dad! My dad's right at the front! Hey, Dad, Dad, here I am!'

Then all the children rushed to the gap in the curtains, sticking their heads out and peering.

All the children except me.

I hung back. I thought of all those chairs, row after row to the back of the hall. I thought of my mum. I willed her to be sitting there right at the front, but *not* next to Justine's dad. I wanted her to be there so much it was as if I had laser eyes that could bore right through the thick crimson velvet. There she was, sitting on the edge of her seat, smiling, waving, her pink heart gleaming round her neck . . .

I had to have one little look. Just to make sure.

I elbowed Justine Big-Bottom Littlewood out of the way and put one eye to the gap between the curtains. The hall was absolutely heaving, with almost every seat taken. I saw all the parents and the wriggly little brothers and sisters. I saw Jenny and Mike. I saw Elaine. She'd taken off her antlers but she had a sprig of mistletoe tied rakishly over one ear (who would want to kiss *Elaine*?). I saw Cam shunting along the front row, finished with her make-up session, every last member of the cast pansticked into character. I saw Justine's awful dad with his gold medallion and his tight leather jacket. I saw everyone . . . except my mum.

I looked right along every single row. She wasn't there. She wasn't in the front. She wasn't in the middle. She wasn't at the back.

Maybe she'd got held up. She'd be jumping out of her stretch limo right this minute, running precariously in her high heels, teeter-tottering up the school drive and now here she was . . .

Not yet.

Any second now.

I stared and stared and stared.

Then I felt a hand on my shoulder.

'Get into place on stage, Tracy. We're about to start,' Miss Simpkins said softly.

'But my mum hasn't come yet! Can't we wait five minutes more? I don't want her to miss the beginning.'

'We'll wait one minute then. You go and settle yourself in your counting-house chair. I'll go and get the carol singers assembled. Then we'll *have* to start, sweetheart.'

'I can't. Not without my mum.'

'You're going to have to, Tracy. The show must

138

go on,' said Miss Simpkins.

I didn't care about the show now. There wasn't any point acting Scrooge if my mum couldn't see me. I clutched my chest. It really hurt. Maybe it was my heart breaking.

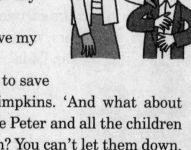

'I couldn't act to save my life,' I said.

'What about acting to save *my* life?' said Miss Simpkins. 'And what about Cam? What about little Peter and all the children who signed his petition? You can't let them down, Tracy.'

I knew she was right. I swallowed very very very hard to get rid of the lump in my throat. I blinked very very very hard to get rid of the water in my eyes. I took a deep deep deep breath.

'Bah!' I said. 'Humbug!'

Miss Simpkins gave me a thumbs-up and then beetled off to cue the carol singers. I sat in my chair, hunched up. They started singing 'Once in Royal David's City'. I started singing my own mournful little version:

'Once in poxy London city
Stood a lowly primary school
Where this girl waits for her mother
To come and see her act the fool.
Carly is that mother wild
Tracy Beaker is that child.'

Then the curtains parted with a swish, the lights went on dimly to show my candle-lit counting house, and I sat tensely in my chair, scowling.

I hated the noise of the chirpy carol singers. All *their* mums and dads were watching them, oohing and aahing and whispering, 'Ah, *bless*.'

My mum wasn't there. She couldn't be bothered to come, even though I'd bought her all those presents. She didn't care tuppence about me.

Well, I didn't care tuppence about her. I didn't care tuppence about *anyone*. I stomped to the side of the stage and shook my fist at the carol singers as they all cried, 'Happy Christmas!'

'Bah!' I said. 'Humbug. Be off with you!'

I felt as if I'd truly turned into Scrooge. My nephew came to wish me Merry Christmas and I sent him off with a flea in his ear. I didn't want to make merry with him. I bullied my stupid clerk Bob Cratchit, and then had a bite to eat. I ate my chicken drumstick like a finicky old man, and when one of the little kids played being a dog on all fours I snatched the bone away and shook my fist at him. He growled at me and I growled back. I heard the audience laugh. Someone whispered, 'Isn't that Tracy Beaker a proper caution!'

Then I went to bed and Justine Enemy-For-Ever Littlewood clanked on stage as Marley's Ghost, the coffin bandage round her head, her long chain trailing keys and padlocks and coinboxes.

Justine's ridiculous dad started clapping wildly before she'd so much as opened her mouth and Justine Utterly-Unprofessional Littlewood totally forgot she was Marley's Ghost. She turned and waved excitedly at her father, just like a five-year-old in her first Nativity play.

I gave a gasp to remind Justine she was there to spook me out and give me a warning. Justine shuffled towards me unwillingly, still peering round at her dad. Her chain tangled around her feet. She wasn't looking where she was going. Recipe for disaster!

Justine tripped over her own padlock and went flying, landing flat on her face.

She lay there, looking a total idiot. Her face was all screwed up. She was trying not to cry.

My chest hurt. I knew just how she felt, falling over and making such a fool of herself in front of her dad. I reached out a shaking hand.

'Is it you, Jacob Marley, my old partner? It *can't* be you, because you're as dead as a doornail.' That was in Miss Simpkins's script. Now it was time for a spot of improvisation. 'Yet it must be you, Marley. You were unsteady on your feet in your last few years on earth – and you're unsteady now in your present spirit situation. Allow me to assist you, old chap.'

I took hold of Justine and hauled her up. The audience clapped delightedly because I'd saved the situation.

'Pray tell me why you're fettered,' I said, following the script again.

'I wear the chain I forged in life,' said Justine, pulling herself together. She sounded pretty miserable, but that was in character.

Then I was visited by Louise as the Spirit of Christmas Past. She'd put her own make-up on over Cam's so she looked more like she was going out clubbing than off haunting mean old men, but at least she didn't fall over.

We acted out the bit where little boy Scrooge was sent to a horrible boarding school and told he couldn't ever go home. It was a bit like me being sent off to the Dumping Ground.

I thought about Mum sending me there and not coming back to fetch me. Not even coming today, when I was starring as Scrooge. Tears rolled down my cheeks. I don't ever cry. But I wasn't being Tracy Beaker; I was acting Scrooge, and doing it so well I heard several snuffles in the audience. They were moved to tears too by my brilliant performance!

144

I had a chance to blow my nose on my nightshirt hem while everyone danced at the Fezziwigs' party. Then the curtains closed and the carol singers stood in front and sang 'Away in a Manger'.

I sang my own version to myself:

'*Away in a schoolhouse*
No mum watched her daughter
But Little Tracy Beaker
Acted incredibly – she didn't falter!'

Miss Simpkins and a host of little helpers rushed round the stage scattering real holly and ivy and mistletoe and fake painted plaster turkeys, ham, mince pies and clementines.

Then the curtains opened and I peered out, waving the carol singers away and going 'Ssh! Ssh!' to the audience. Fat Freddy waddled on stage in his Father Christmas outfit as the Spirit of Christmas Present and took me to see the Cratchit family.

Peter was shaking all over, scared out of his wits, but the moment he hopped across the stage using his crutch everyone went 'Aaah! Doesn't he look *sweet*!' When he said, 'God bless us every one,' they all started clapping.

It looked as if weedy little Peter had stolen the show.

It was *my* show. I was Scrooge. I wanted them just to clap *me*. But Peter was my friend. He'd tried so hard for me. My chest hurt again. He liked me so much. And I liked him. I really did. Maybe I was a little bit glad he was being such a success. When the Spirit of Christmas Present told me Tiny Tim was going to die I cried straight from the heart, 'No, no! Oh no, kind Spirit! Say he will be spared!'

Then, as midnight struck, I spotted the two tiny children hiding under the Spirit's robes, the smallest skinniest kids Miss Simpkins could find, one playing Ignorance and one playing Want.

The last Spirit came creeping onto the stage,

draped in a long black robe, the scary Spirit of Christmas Yet to Come. The lights were very low so it looked as if we were wandering through the night together. We went to the Cratchit house, so melancholy without Tiny Tim. Then we went to the graveyard. Miss Simpkins shone a torch on the great cardboard tombstone. I saw my own name written there, Ebenezer Scrooge. I trembled and threw myself down on my knees.

'Oh, Spirit, have mercy!' I cried. 'Tell me I can sponge away the writing on this stone. I have learned my lesson. I will honour Christmas in my heart and try to keep it all the year.'

Then the lights went out and I jumped into my own bed quick as a wink and then acted waking up on Christmas Day. The carol signers sang 'We Wish You a Merry Christmas' outside my window. I sprang out of bed, did a little caper in my nightgown, and then went and called out to them.

'I wish you a Merry Christmas too, dear fellows. A Merry Christmas and a Happy New Year, and I, Ebenezer Scrooge, am going to lead a happy new life.'

Bells rang out and I danced up and down. Then I put my coat on over my nightshirt and rushed off stage, staggering back with the most comically enormous turkey, almost as big as me. I invited everyone to my house for Christmas. The whole cast crammed on stage and we 'ate' plastic mince pies and quaffed pretend wine – even Marley's Ghost and the three Christmas Spirits – and then we all sang 'God Rest Ye Merry Gentlemen'.

God rest ye merry gentlemen, let nothing you dismay...

I got Peter to shout out, 'God bless us every one!' right at the end.

Then the clapping started. It went on and on and on. We all stood holding hands and bowing. The four Ghosts got a special bow. Then Peter had to bow all by himself. He was so excited he did a little hoppy dance, waving his crutch, and the audience roared.

Then it was my turn. I stood in front of all the others. Cam and Jenny and Mike and Elaine stood up and started clapping and clapping. Miss Simpkins at the side of the stage was clapping and clapping. *Mrs Darlow* at the back of the hall was clapping and clapping. All the mums and dads were clapping and clapping.

But my mum wasn't clapping. She wasn't there.

It was the proudest moment of my life. I'd acted Scrooge and I'd been *good* at it. Glorious. Magnificent. The audience shouted '*Bravo!*' And '*Good for Tracy!*' And '*What a little star!*'

Mum didn't know. Mum didn't care.

I had a smile all over my face and yet my eyes were going blink blink blink. I was in serious danger of having an attack of hay fever in front of everyone.

Miss Simpkins came out onto the stage holding an enormous bunch of red roses and white lilies done up with a huge red satin ribbon.

'They've just arrived, Tracy. They're for you,'
she said, handing them over.

There was a card inside.

Congratulations, my little star.
Wish I could have seen you.
Lots of love, mum xxx

'It's from my *mum*!' I said – but the note
proved *fatal* for my hay fever. Still, everyone
knows flowers trigger hay-fever attacks. I wasn't
crying. I don't *ever* cry.

Then we had a proper party in the hall with
real mince pies for everyone. Cam came and
hugged me hard and said she was so very proud
of me.

'You were totally brilliant, Tracy,' she said.
'And there's you saying you couldn't remember
a word!'

'Well, it didn't *feel* as if I was remembering it.

It wasn't like *acting*. It was as if I was really living it,' I said.

'Aha! That shows you're a *real* actor,' said Cam.

'Like Mum,' I said.

'Just like your mum.' Cam smiled at me. 'Aren't they gorgeous flowers? Wasn't it lovely of her to send them? Imagine, getting your own huge bouquet of flowers.'

'Yeah. With a lovely note. Did you see what my mum wrote?'

'Yes, Tracy.'

'The only thing is . . .' I swallowed. 'It's not my mum's handwriting.'

I looked hard at Cam. She didn't look away. She stared straight into my eyes.

'Of course it's not your mum's actual writing, Tracy. You order the flowers on the phone and say what you want on the card and then the local florist writes it down.'

'Oh!' I said. I swallowed again. The mince pie seemed made of very lumpy pastry. 'You wouldn't kid me, would you, Cam?'

152

'No one could ever kid you, Tracy Beaker,' said Cam.

'Well, I think it was lovely of my mum. But it would have been a lot lovelier if she'd actually come to see me,' I said.

'I'm sure she would have done if she possibly could,' said Cam.

'Do you think she's still coming to see me on Christmas Day?' I said.

'Well . . . maybe she is,' said Cam.

'And maybe she's not,' I said. 'So what am I going to do on Christmas Day, eh? I *hate* Christmas in the Dumping Ground. Jenny and Mike try hard but they've always got the little kids clinging to them and everyone tears open their presents too quickly and then fusses because they think the others have got better things, and there's never enough new batteries and often the stuff doesn't work anyway. We watch television but all the programmes are about families and we are all so *not* a family. We have turkey and Christmas pudding for dinner because Jenny wants it to be traditional so we don't miss out, but I don't really *like* turkey or Christmas pudding – though I eat too much anyway – and then we're supposed to play these crazy games but the little kids are too dim to play and the big kids just want to slope off to their rooms and someone always throws a tantrum because they're so fed up and lonely and left out. That someone is quite often me, as a matter of fact.'

'Hmm,' said Cam. 'It sounds as if we both have crap Christmases. Tell you what, Tracy. Let's join up together. You come to me for Christmas. What do you think?'

'I think that sounds a brilliant idea,' I said.

So that's exactly what I did. I woke up very early on Christmas morning and opened all my presents peacefully, all by myself. Jenny gave me cool new jeans and a CD and Mike gave me new trainers and amazing black nail varnish. Elaine gave me a *little fluffy blue teddy bear* – yuck yuck yuck! Peter gave me a silver yo-yo. It was very sweet of him. I decided to give him the blue teddy.

My mum didn't give me anything.

I expect the roses and lilies cost a lot of money. Acting is a chancy profession. Maybe Mum was a bit strapped for cash at the moment.

Of course, Grizelda Moonbeam might work her magic and Mum might appear in person, weighed down with presents. But somehow it wasn't starting to seem very likely. It didn't look as if I was going to be spending this festive occasion with my Loved One. Unless . . . maybe *Cam* counted as a Loved One? Was I *her* Loved One?? Had the charm actually worked a double whammy???

I knew Cam was certainly short of money so I wasn't too hopeful about her present to me. She arrived astonishingly early. She was wearing a woolly hat and scarf and mittens, with a big woolly jumper over her jeans and woolly socks.

'Happy Christmas, Cam! Have you got woolly *knickers* on? Why are you all bundled up? And you're so *early*. We haven't even had breakfast yet. Do you want some?'

'Happy Christmas, Tracy. You need to pile on lots of woolly jumpers too. We're going for a walk. And we're having breakfast out, OK?'

She drove us for miles to this big park. It wasn't snowing but it was still early enough for there to be a frost so we could kid ourselves it was a real white Christmas.

'Come on!' said Cam, parking the car. She opened the door. It certainly *felt* frosty. I hadn't got quite enough woollies.

'It's freezing, Cam! Can't we stay in the car?'

'We're going for a walk, Tracy, to work up an appetite for our breakfast.'

'You go for a walk. I'll stay in the car and watch you,' I said.

She dragged me out, rammed her own woolly hat over my head, wound her scarf round and round and round me as if she was wrapping a mummy, and then took me by the hand.

'There! Cosy now? Off we go!'

'I'm not really *into* long country walks, Cam. I'm not built for it. Look at my spindly legs.' I made my knees knock together and walked with a Tiny Tim limp.

'Just come down this path with me,' said Cam, tugging me. 'Through the trees. You'll like what you see when you get to the end.'

I knew what I'd see. *Scenery*. A lot more trees and a hill or two. I didn't see the point. Still, it was Christmas after all. I didn't want to be too difficult. I sighed and staggered after Cam. I didn't get why she wanted to stay out in the cold, especially before breakfast.

'I don't want to moan, but my tummy's rumbling rather a lot. It's saying, *Tracy, Tracy, what's happened to my cornflakes?*'

'You'll have breakfast very soon, I promise,' said Cam, laughing.

'Are we having a picnic then?' I asked.

It seemed a mad time of year to have a picnic and I didn't see any signs of a hamper. Cam wasn't carrying so much as a lunch box. Perhaps she had a sandwich or two crammed in her pockets? It looked like it was going to be a very *little* picnic, yet I was totally *starving*.

Cam and I weren't the only ones embarking

on this mad early-morning Starve-In. There were lots of other cars in the car park and little bunches of bobble-hatted muffled weirdos trudged along too, all heading in the same direction. It was like we were all in *Doctor Who* and some alien force was messing with our heads, controlling our minds.

Then we rounded a bend. I saw a big pond in the distance. A lot of people were *in* the pond. No, no, they were *on* it, gliding across.

'They're skating!' I said.

'Yep.'

'Can *we* skate?'

'We'll have a go.'

'But we haven't got any skates.'

'You can hire them, Tracy, I checked. And they're serving a special Christmas breakfast.'

'Oh, wow! So you planned it all? Oh, Cam, you have some seriously cool ideas.'

I gave her a quick hug and then started running helter-skelter to the ice. There was a big van serving golden croissants and hot chocolate with whipped cream. We had breakfast first, just to fortify ourselves, and then we hired our skates, held hands and hobbled onto the ice.

I thought I'd glide off like a swan, swoop-swoop, swirl-swirl, the epitome of athletic grace. Ha! I staggered like a drunk, clonk-clunk, whizz, whoops, bonk on my bum. Cam pulled me up, trying not to laugh.

'Look, Tracy, point your boots out and do it like *this*,' she said, demonstrating.

Some kid hurtled past her, making her jump. She wavered, wobbled – and then went bonk on *her* bum.

I *did* laugh and Cam laughed too.

'I don't know about woolly knickers. I think we both need *padded* knickers,' she said as I pulled her up.

We held onto each other and tried again. This time we staggered all the way round the pond. I started to get more daring. I tried a little swoop.

It worked! I tried another – left, right, truly gliding – only I couldn't seem to stop. I went charging straight into a little cluster of kids in a line and mowed them all down.

'We're going to have to rename you Tracy Bulldozer,' said Cam, hauling us all up.

We skated for over an hour, losing count of the number of times we both fell over, but we could also both glide properly for a few seconds at a time, so considered ourselves champion skaters.

'I think we deserve another breakfast after all that effort,' said Cam, and we polished off *another* croissant and mug of hot chocolate.

160

Then Cam drove us back to her house. She had a little Christmas tree in her living room.

'I usually don't bother, but they were selling them half price in the market yesterday so I decided to go mad.'

'It looks a bit naked if you don't mind me saying so. Aren't you meant to have little glass balls and tinsel and fairy lights?' I said.

'Of course you are. I thought it would be fun if we decorated the tree together,' said Cam. 'Look in that big carrier bag. There's all the decorations.'

'Oh, fantastic! We don't have a proper tree at the Dumping Ground because the little kids are so dopey they might mistake the glass balls for apples and the big kids are so rowdy they might knock it all over. I've *always* wanted to decorate a tree!'

'Then be my guest. I'll go and sort out what we might be having for Christmas dinner. I know you don't go a bundle on turkey and I'm mostly veggie nowadays . . . I could do a sort of tofu and vegetable casserole?'

'That sounds absolutely temptingly delicious – *not*!' I said.

'I rather thought that would be your response. I don't fancy faffing around in the kitchen for hours anyway. How about egg and chips?'

'Now you're talking! With lots of tomato sauce?'

'You can dollop it all over your plate, Tracy. It's Christmas. Ah! What else do you get at Christmas? We've got a Christmas tree. We'll have our Christmas dinner. But there's something else you have at Christmas. Um. What could it be? Oh yes! Presents!'

She opened up a cupboard and pulled out three parcels in jolly Santa wrapping paper tied with red ribbon.

'Oh, Cam! Are they for me?'

'Well, they've all got Tracy Beaker on the labels, so if that's your name I'd say it was a safe bet they're all for you.'

I felt really really really great. Cam had bought me loads of lovely presents.

162

I felt really really really bad. I hadn't got Cam anything.

'Oh dear, why the saddo face? Did you hope there might be more?' Cam teased.

'*You* haven't got any presents, Cam!' I wailed.

'Yes I have. I've opened mine already. I got a silk *headscarf* from my mum – as if I'd ever wear it! Plus a posh credit-card holder when I'm so overdrawn I can't use my blooming cards anyway. I got lovely presents from my friends though. Jane gave me my woolly hat and scarf and mittens and Liz gave me a big box of chocs and a book token.'

'What's a book *token*?'

'It's a little card for a certain amount of money and when you take it to a shop you can change it for any book you fancy.'

'Oh, I get it.' I nodded. 'Good idea!'

'Come on then, open your presents from me.'

I opened the heaviest first. It was ten children's paperbacks. They were all a bit dog-eared and tattered.

'I'm afraid they're second-hand,' said Cam. 'I searched in all the charity shops. A lot of them were ten-pence bargains!'

163

I eyed them suspiciously. 'They're classics,' I said. 'Aren't they, like, boring?'

'Is *A Christmas Carol* boring? No! These were all my favourites when I was your age. Cam Lawson's Top Ten Super Reads for kids your age. If you don't want them I'll have a great time re-reading them. *Little Women* is about this family of sisters and they like acting too, and reading Charles Dickens. You'll especially like Jo, who's a tomboy and wants to be a writer.

'Then there's *Black Beauty*. It's a wonderful story, and there's a very sad bit about a horse called Ginger which always makes me cry, but it's lovely all the same. *What Katy Did* is about a big family – Katy's the eldest, and she's always in heaps of trouble but then she falls off a swing and can't walk for ages. She's got a very saintly cousin who irritates a bit, but it's a great story, truly.

'*The Wind in the Willows* is about a mole

and a rat who are great chums and
they have this pal Toad who's a
terrible show-off, and there are some
very funny bits. *Five Children and It*
is also funny – it's about these kids who
meet a sand fairy and all their wishes come
true, but they always go wrong.'

'Chance would be a fine thing,' I said,
sniffing.

'There's also *Mary Poppins*. The book's
much better than the film. I loved *Tom
Sawyer* because he's very badly behaved
and always in trouble, and you might give
Anne of Green Gables a go. It's all about
this little orphan girl who won't ever
stop talking. You'll identify big-time
with those two.

'I'm sure you'll like *The Secret
Garden* because Mary is wondrously
grouchy and rude to everyone and has
to live in a house with a hundred rooms
on the Yorkshire Moors. And
Ballet Shoes is a perfect
book for you, because these
three sisters go to a stage
school and perform in lots

of plays, and I think that's maybe what you might end up doing, Tracy.'

'OK, OK. I'll give them a go,' I said. 'I can always share them with some of the other kids, eh? Peter might like the Mole and Rat and Toad book.'

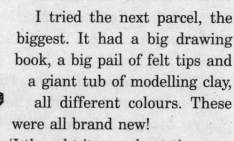

I tried the next parcel, the biggest. It had a big drawing book, a big pail of felt tips and a giant tub of modelling clay, all different colours. These were all brand new!

'I thought it was about time you had your own art supplies instead of raiding poor Elaine's art cupboard,' said Cam.

'Oh wow! I'm *not* going to share these!'

Finally I picked up the tiniest parcel. I unwrapped it and found a little black box. I opened it up – and there was a silver star pin badge.

'It's for you, Tracy Beaker Superstar,' said Cam, pinning it on me.

I gave her a big big big hug.

Then I decorated the tree, carefully dangling each glass ball and chocolate Santa and little bird and twirly glass icicle, while Cam wound the fairy lights round and round. When we switched them on the tree looked totally magical.

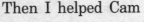

Then I helped Cam cook the lunch. She got me peeling potatoes. I had no idea that was the real way to make chips. Ours come in giant packets at the Dumping Ground, already peeled and sliced. I started peeling pounds of potatoes, whistling as I whittled.

'Steady on, girl. There's just the two of us,' said Cam.

'I never get quite *enough* chips at the Dumping Ground,' I said.

'OK. It's Christmas. Today you can eat until you burst,' said Cam.

She wouldn't let me fry them in the big

sizzling chip pan, but she *did* let me
fry our eggs and that was great fun.
We both had *enormous* piles
of golden chips on our
plates, with a fried egg
on top like snow on
a mountain peak.
I squirted mine
liberally with scarlet
sauce and then we
started eating. I ate
and ate and ate. My meal was delicious.

'I make the most excellent egg and chips ever,'
I said, licking my lips. 'Maybe I'm going to be a
famous chef as well as a brilliant writer and a
superstar actress.'

Cam ate her chips valiantly but had to give
up halfway through. We had clementines for
pudding, then Cam opened up her big box of
chocolates from Liz and we snaffled some of
those.

Then Cam undid her jeans and lay on the sofa,
groaning, while I got my new art stuff and started
creating. Cam rubbed her tummy, reached for a
book and started reading me the first Christmasy
chapter of *Little Women*. It was quite good in

an old-fashioned sort of way. Meg was a bit of a goody-goody and Beth was a bit wet and Amy was too pert and girly but I *loved* Jo.

Cam's voice tailed away after a while and she dozed off. I carried on and on and on creating. Then, when she started yawning and stretching and opening her eyes, I went and made her a cup of tea. No one has ever shown me how to do it but I'm not a total moron.

'Thank you, Tracy!' said Cam. She took a sip. 'Delicious!'

(I spotted her fishing several of the teabags out of her cup and spooning out a few of the still melting sugar lumps, but neither of us mentioned this.)

'I've got you some Christmas presents after all,' I said. 'Look on your coffee table.' I pointed proudly.

Cam nearly spilled her tea. 'Oh my lord! Multiple Tracy Beakers!' she said.

'Aren't they great!' I said. 'I made them with my modelling clay. The pink face was fine, and the red jumper and the blue skirt, but making my black curls all squiggly took *ages*.'

'Are all six for me?' said Cam.

'No, no. You have *this* one. She's the best, with the biggest smile. And I've got one for Peter and one for Jenny and one for Mike, and I suppose I ought to give one to Elaine and I thought I'd give one to Miss Simpkins when I go back to school.'

'That's a lovely idea. Well, I shall treasure my Tracy Beaker model. I'll put her on my desk. She can keep me company when I'm writing.'

'Don't crumple her up by mistake if you get stuck!' I said. 'Look, you've got another present.'

I handed her a folded piece of paper with a picture of me on the front.

'Oh, a card. How lovely!' said Cam.

'It's not a card. It's a Tracy token,' I said. 'You know, like a book token. But you don't get books with this token, you get *me*. Look inside.'

I'd written:

To Cam. Happy Christmas! 🌿

I, Tracy Beaker, promise to make you a plate of my famous egg and chips whenever I'm round at your place. 🍳 I will make you DOUBLE egg and chips on your birthday. 🍳

If I get to be a famous chef with my own swanky restaurant I will create a famous egg and chips dish and call it my <u>Cam Christmas Special.</u>

If I get to be a famous writer I will dedicate my second book to you. I hope that's okay, but I have to dedicate my first book to my mum.

If I get to be a famous superstar actress I will let you be my drama coach. 😄 😩

And if you finish your classes and go through with fostering me I will be the best foster daughter ever.

Love from

Tracy

xxx

Cam read it through, sniffling. 'Oh, Tracy,' she said. 'This is the best Christmas present I've ever had. And of course you'll be the best foster-daughter ever. You're *Tracy Beaker*.'

Yes I am. Tracy Beaker Superstar.

When I went to bed that night back at the Dumping Ground I gave Mum's photo a kiss.

'I hope you had a Happy Christmas, Mum,' I whispered. 'Maybe see you next year, yeah?'

Then I lay back in bed and sang a little Christmas carol to myself.

'*Silent night, holy night,*
Tracy is calm, Tracy is bright.
Mum didn't come but I had a good time,
I love Mum but I'm glad Cam is mine.
Now I'll sleep in heavenly peace,
S-l-e-e-p in heav-en-ly peeeace.'

Turn the page to read the brilliant
first chapter of the next installment
in Tracy Beaker's story,

The Dare Game

No Home

You know that old film they always show on the telly at Christmas, *The Wizard of Oz*? I love it, especially the Wicked Witch of the West with her cackle and her green face and all her special flying monkeys. I'd give anything to have a wicked winged monkey as an evil little pet. It could whiz through the sky, flapping its wings and sniffing the air for that awful stale instant-coffee-and-talcum-powder *teacher* smell and then it would s-w-o-o-p straight onto Mrs Vomit Bagley and carry her away screaming.

That'll show her. I've always been absolutely Tip Top at writing stories, but since I've been at this stupid new school Mrs V.B. just puts *'Disgracefully untidy work, Tracy'* and *'Check your spellings!'* Last week we had to write a story about 'Night-time' and I thought it an unusually cool subject so I wrote eight and a half pages about this girl out late at night and it's seriously spooky and then this crazy guy jumps out at her and almost murders her but she escapes by jumping in the river and then she swims right into this bloated corpse and *then* when she staggers onto the bank there's this strange flickering light coming from the nearby graveyard and it's an evil occult sect wanting to sacrifice an innocent young girl and she's *just* what they're looking for . . .

It's a truly GREAT story, better than any that Cam could write. (I'll tell you about Cam in a minute.) I'm sure it's practically good enough to get published. I typed it out on Cam's computer so it looked ever so neat and the spellcheck took care of all the spellings so I was all prepared for Mrs V.B. to bust a gut and write: '*Very very very good indeed, Tracy. 10 out of 10 and Triple Gold Star and I'll buy you a tube of Smarties at playtime.*'

Do you know what she really wrote? '*You've tried hard, Tracy, but this is a very rambling story. You also have a very warped imagination!*'

I looked up 'warp' in the dictionary she's always recommending and it means 'to twist out of shape'. That's spot on. I'd like to warp Mrs Vomit Bagley, twisting and twisting, until her eyes pop and her arms and legs are wrapped right round her great big bum. That's another thing. Whenever I write the weeniest babiest little rude word Mrs V.B. goes bananas. I don't know what she'd do if I used *really* bad words like **** and **** and ****** (censored!!).

I looked up 'ramble' too. I liked what it said: 'To stroll about freely, as for relaxation, with no particular direction'. So that's *exactly* what I did today, instead of staying at boring old school. I bunked off and strolled round the town freely, as relaxed as anything. I had a little potter in Paperchase and bought this big fat purple notebook with my pocket money. I'm going to write all my mega-manic ultra-scary stories in it, as warped and as rambly as I can make them. And I'll write *my* story too. I've written all about myself before in *The Story of Tracy Beaker*. So this can be *The Story of Tracy Beaker Two* or *Find Out What Happens Next to the Brave and Brilliant Tracy Beaker* or *Further Fabulous Adventures of the Tremendous Terrific Tracy Beaker* or *Read More About the Truly Terrible Tracy Beaker, Even More Wicked Than the Wicked Witch of the West*.

Yes. I was telling you about *The Wizard of Oz*. There's only one bit that I truly dread. I can't actually watch it. The first time I saw it I very nearly cried. (I *don't* cry, though. I'm tough. As old boots. New boots. The biggest fiercest reinforced Doc Martens . . .) It's the bit right at the end where Dorothy is getting fed up with being in Oz. Which is mad, if you ask me. Who'd want to go back to that boring black and white Kansas and be an ordinary kid where they take your dog away when you could dance round Oz in your ruby slippers? But Dorothy acts in an extremely dumb manner all the way through the film. You'd think she'd have sussed out for herself that all she had to do was click those ruby slippers and she'd get back home. That's it. That's the bit. Where she says, 'There's no place like home.'

It gets to me. Because there's no place like home for me. No place at all. I haven't got a home.

Well. I didn't have up until recently. Unless you count the Home. If a home has a capital letter at the front you can be pretty sure it isn't like a *real* home. It's just a dumping ground for kids with problems. The ugly kids, the bad kids, the daft kids. The ones no-one wants to foster. The kids way past their sell-by date so they're all chucked on the rubbish heap. There were certainly some ultra-rubbishy kids at that Home. Especially a certain Justine Littlewood ...

We were Deadly Enemies once, but then we made up. I even gave Justine my special Mickey Mouse pen. I rather regretted this actually and asked for it back the next day, pretending it had just been a loan, but Justine wasn't having any. There are no flies on Justine. No wasps, bees or any kind of bug.

It's weird, but I kind of miss Justine now. It was even fun when we were Deadly Enemies and we played the Dare Game. I've always been great at thinking up the silliest daftest rudest dares. I always dared everything and won until Justine came to the Children's Home. Then I *still* won. Most of the time. I *did*. But Justine could certainly invent some seriously wicked dares herself.

I miss her. I miss Louise too. And I especially miss Peter. This is even weirder. I couldn't stand weedy old Peter when he first came to the Home. But now it feels like he was my best ever friend. I wish I could see him. I especially wish I could see him right now. Because I'm all on my own and although it's great to be bunking off school and I've found the most brilliant hiding place in the whole world it is a little bit lonely.

I could do with a mate. When you're in care you need to make all the friends you can get because you don't have much family.

Well. I've got family.

I've got the loveliest prettiest best-ever mum in the whole world. She's this dead famous Hollywood movie star and she's in film after film, in so much demand that there isn't a minute of the day when she can see me so that's why I'm in care . . .

Who am I kidding??? Not you. Not even me. I used to carry on like that when I was little, and some kids took it all in and even acted like they were impressed. But now when I come out with all that movie guff they start to get this little curl of the lip and then the minute my back's turned I hear a splutter of laughter. And that's the *kinder* kids. The rest tell me straight to my face that I'm a nutter. They don't even believe my mum's an actress. I know for a fact she's been in *some* films. She sent me this big glossy photo of her in this negligée – but now kids nudge and giggle and say, 'What *kind* of film was your mum in, Tracy Beaker?'

So I duff them up. Sometimes literally. I'm very handy with my fists. Sometimes I just pretend it in my head. I should have pretended inside my head with Mrs Vomit Bagley. It isn't wise to tell teachers exactly what you think of them. She gave us this new piece of writing work this morning. About 'My Family'. It was supposed to be an exercise in autobiography. It's really a way for the teachers to be dead nosy and find out all sorts of secrets about the kids. Anyway, after she's told us all to start writing this 'My Family' stuff she squeezes her great hips in and out the desks till she gets to me. She leans over until her face is hovering a few inches from mine. I thought for one seriously scary second she was going to *kiss* me!

'Of course, *you* write about your foster mother, Tracy,' she whispers, her Tic-Tac minty breath tickling my ear.

She thought she was whispering discreetly, but every single kid in the room looked up and stared. So I stared straight back and edged as far away from Mrs V.B. as I could and said firmly, 'I'm going to write about my *real* mother, Mrs Bagley.'

So I did. Page after page. My writing got a bit sprawly and I gave up on spelling and stopped bothering about full stops and capital letters because they're such a waste of time, but I wrote this *amazing* account of me and my mum. Only I never finished it. Because Mrs V.B. does another Grand Tour of the class, bending over and reading your work over your shoulder in the most off-putting way possible, and she gets to me and leans over, and then she sniffs inwards and sighs. I thought she was just going to have the usual old nag about Neatness and Spelling and Punctuation — but this time she was miffed about the content, not the presentation.

'You and your extraordinary imagination, Tracy,' she said, in this falsely sweet patronizing tone. She even went 'Tut tut', shaking her head, still with this silly smirk on her face.

'What do you mean?' I said, sharpish.

'Tracy! Don't take that rude tone with me, dear.' There was an edge to her voice and all. 'I did my best to explain about Autobiography. It means you tell a *true* story about yourself and your own life.'

'It *is* true. All of it,' I said indignantly.

'Really, Tracy!' she said, and she started reading bits out, not trying to keep her voice down now, revving up for public proclamation.

'"My mum is starring in a Hollywood movie with George Clooney and Tom Cruise and Brad Pitt and they all think she's wonderful and want to be her boyfriend. Her new movie is going to star Leonardo DiCaprio as her younger brother and she's got really matey with Leonardo at rehearsals and he's seen the photo of me she carries around in her wallet and he says I look real cute and wants to write to me,"' Mrs V.B. read out in this poisonous high-pitched imitation of my voice.

The entire class collapsed. Some of the kids practically wet themselves laughing. Mrs V.B. had this smirk puckering her lips. 'Do you really believe this, Tracy?' she asked.

So I said, 'I really believe that you're a stupid hideous old bag who could only get a part in a movie about bloodsucking vampire bats.'

I thought for a moment she was going to prove her bat-star qualities by flying at my neck and biting me with her fangs. She certainly wanted to. But she just marched me out of the room instead and told me to stand outside the door because she was sick of my insolence.

I said she made *me* sick and it was a happy chance that her name was Mrs V. Bagley. The other kids might wonder whether the V. stood for Vera or Violet or Vanessa, but I was certain her first name was Vomit, and dead appropriate too, given her last name, because she looked like the contents of a used vomit bag.

She went back into the classroom when I was only halfway through so I said it to myself, slumping against the wall and staring at my shoes. I said I was Thrilled to Bits to miss out on her lesson because she was boring boring boring and couldn't teach for toffee. She couldn't teach for fudge, nougat, licorice or Turkish delight. I declared I was utterly Ecstatic to be Outside.

Then Mr Hatherway walked past with a little squirt from Year Three with a nosebleed. 'Talking to yourself, kiddo?' he said.

'No, I'm talking to my shoes,' I said crossly.

I expected him to have a go at me too but he just nodded and mopped the little spurting scarlet fountain. 'I have a quiet chat to *my* shoes when things are getting me down,' he said. 'Very understanding friends, shoes. I find my old Hush Puppies especially comforting.'

The little squirt gave a whimper and Mr Hatherway gave him another mop. 'Come on, pal, we'd better get you some first aid.'

He gave me a little nod and they walked on. Up until that moment I was convinced that this new school was 100% horrible. Now it was maybe 1% OK, because I quite liked Mr Hatherway. Not that I had any chance of having him as my teacher, not unless I was shoved out of Year Six right to the bottom of the Juniors. And the school was still 99% the pits, so I decided to clear off out of it.

It was easy-peasy. I waited till playtime

when Mrs V.B. waved me away, her nostrils pinched like I smelled bad. So I returned the compliment and held my own nose but she pretended not to notice. It was music in the hall with Miss Smith after playtime so I was someone else's responsibility then. Only I wasn't going to stick around for music because Miss Smith keeps picking on me too, just because of that one time I experimented with alternative uses of a drumstick. So I moseyed down the corridor like I was going to the toilets only I went right on walking, round the corner, extra sharpish past Reception (though Mrs Ludovic was busy mopping the little kid with the nosebleed. It looked like World War Three in her office) and then quick out the door and off across the yard. The main gate was locked but that presented no problem at all for SuperTracy. I was up that wall and over in a flash. I did fall over the other side and both my knees got a bit chewed up but that didn't bother me.

They hurt quite a lot now, even though they've stopped bleeding. They both look pretty dirty. I've probably introduced all sorts of dangerous germs into my bloodstream and any minute now I'll develop a high fever and start frothing at the mouth. I don't feel very well actually. And I'm *starving*. I wish I hadn't spent all my money on this notebook. I especially wish I hadn't picked one the exact purple of a giant bar of Cadbury's milk chocolate. I shall start slavering all over it soon.

I'd really like to call it a day and push off back to Cam's but the clock's just struck and it's only one o'clock. Lunchtime. Only I haven't any lunch. I can't go back till teatime or Cam will get suspicious. I *could* show her my savaged knees and say I had a Dire Accident and got sent home, but Cam would think I'd been fighting again. I got in enough trouble the last time. It wasn't *fair*. I didn't start the fight.

It was all that Roxanne Green's fault. She made this sneery remark to her friends about my T-shirt. She was showing off in her new DKNY T-shirt, zigzagging her shoulders this way and that, so I started imitating her and everyone laughed. So she goes, 'What label is *your* T-shirt, Tracy?'

Before I could make anything up she says, '*I* know. It's Oxfam!'

Everyone laughed again but this time it was awful so I got mad and called Roxanne various names and then she called *me* names and most of it was baby stuff but then she said the B word – and added that it was true in my case because I really didn't have a dad.

So I had to smack her one then, didn't I? It was only fair. Only Roxanne and all her little girly hangers-on didn't think it was fair and they told Mrs Vomit Bagley and she *certainly* didn't think it was fair and she told Mr Donne the headteacher and, guess what, he didn't think it was fair either. He rang Cam and asked her to come to the school for a Quiet Word. I was yanked along to the study too and I said lots of words not at *all* quietly, but Cam put her arm round me and hissed in my ear, 'Cool it, Trace.'

I tried. I thought c-o-o-l and imagined a beautiful blue lake of water and me swimming slowly along – but I was so sizzling mad the water started to bubble all around me and I ended up boiling over and telling the head what I thought of him and his poxy teachers and putrid pupils. (Get my vocabulary, Mrs V.B.!)

I very nearly ended up being excluded. Which is mad. I should have been even cheekier because I don't *want* to go to this terrible old school.

So I've excluded myself.

I'm here.

In my own secret place. Dead exclusive. My very own house.

Home!

Well, it's not exactly *homely* at the moment. It needs a good going over with a vacuum or two. Or three or four or five. And even though it's kind of empty it needs a spot of tidying. There are empty beer cans and McDonald's cartons chucked all over the place, and all kinds of freebie papers and advertising bumpf litter the hall so you're wading ankle-deep when you come in the front door. Only I didn't, seeing as it's locked and bolted and boarded over. I came in the back, through the broken window, ever so carefully.

I went in the back garden because I was mooching round and round the streets, dying for a wee. I came across this obviously empty house down at the end of a little cul-de-sac with big brambles all over the place giving lots of cover so I thought I'd nip over the wall quick and relieve myself. Which I did, though a black cat suddenly streaked past, which made me jump and lose concentration so I very nearly weed all over my trainers.

When I was relieved and decent I tried to catch the cat, pretending this was a jungle and the cat was a tiger and I was all set to train it but the cat went 'Purr-lease!' and stalked off with its tail in the air.

I explored the jungle by myself and spotted the broken window and decided to give the house a recce too.

It's a great house. It hasn't quite got all mod cons any more. The water's been turned off and the lights won't switch on and the radiators are cold. But there's still a sofa in the living room, quite a swish one, red velvet. Some plonker's put his muddy boots all over it, but I've been scratching at it with my fingernails and I think it'll clean up a treat.

I could bring a cushion. And a blanket. And some *food*. Yeah.

Next time.

But now it's time for me to go . . . back to Cam.

ABOUT THE AUTHOR

JACQUELINE WILSON is one of Britain's most outstanding writers for young readers. She is the most borrowed author from British libraries and has sold over 20 million books in this country. As a child, she always wanted to be a writer and wrote her first 'novel' when she was nine, filling countless exercise books as she grew up. She started work at a publishing company and then went on to work as a journalist on *Jackie* magazine (which was named after her) before turning to writing fiction full-time.

Jacqueline has been honoured with many of the UK's top awards for children's books, including the Guardian Children's Fiction Award, the Smarties Prize and the Children's Book of the Year. She was awarded an OBE in 2002 and is the Children's Laureate for 2005-2007.

'A brilliant writer of wit and subtlety whose stories are never patronising and are often complex and many-layered' *The Times*

'It's the combination of accessible stories and humorous but penetrating treatment of big emotional themes that makes this writer so good' *Financial Times*

ABOUT THE ILLUSTRATOR

NICK SHARRATT knew from an early age that
he wanted to use his artistic skills in his career.
He went to Manchester Polytechnic to do an
Art Foundation course, followed by a BA (Hons)
in Graphic Design at St Martin's School of Art
in London. Since graduating in 1984, Nick has
been working full-time as an illustrator, with
his work hugely in demand for children's books.

His famous collaboration with Jacqueline
Wilson began with *The Story of Tracy Beaker*,
published in 1991 and he has illustrated every
one of her best-selling books published by
Doubleday/Corgi since then.

Nick also illustrates full-colour picture and
novelty books, such as *Eat Your Peas* (Bodley Head),
written by Kes Gray, which won the 2000 Children's
Book Award and *Pants* (David Fickling Books),
written by Giles Andreae, which also won the
Children's Book Award and was shortlisted for the
prestigious Kate Greenaway Medal in 2003.
He also writes his own picture books.

Nick lives in Brighton, Sussex.

Join the FREE online

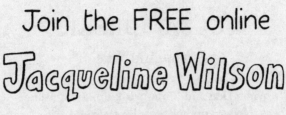

Jacqueline Wilson

☆ FAN CLUB ☆

Read Jacqueline's monthly diary, look up

tour info, receive fan club e-newsletters.

All this and more, including members'

jokes and loads of exclusive top offers

Visit www.jacquelinewilson.co.uk

for more info!

CLEAN BREAK

Jacqueline Wilson

When Dad and Mum break up, Em does her
best to cheer up her little brother and sister, even
though she's miserable too. She dances around
and tells wonderful tales all about their favourite
glove puppet. Em knows how a good story can
make life seem better. She is always cheered
up by reading one of her favourite books. If Em
got to meet the author, it would be a dream
come true. But could her other greatest wish
be granted? Is any story powerful enough
to bring Dad back?

Another wonderful book about real family life
from a prize-winning, best-selling author.

ISBN 978 0 440 86643 5

MIDNIGHT

Jacqueline Wilson

*Fairies steal away beloved babies and leave
a changeling in their place . . .*

Violet has always been in the shadow of her
mesmerising, controlling brother Will – by turns
delightful and terrifying. But now Will has learned
a shocking secret about his own past, and things
seem to be getting worse. Violet retreats into her
fantasies based on the fairy characters created
by her absolute favourite author, Casper Dream.

The arrival of Jasmine, a new girl at school who
immediately befriends Violet, seems like it might
change Violet's life for the better. Will Jasmine
allow her to break free of Will's spell?

A magical and atmospheric novel from
multi-award winner Jacqueline Wilson.

ISBN 978 0 440 86578 0

THE DIAMOND GIRLS

Jacqueline Wilson

'You're all my favourite Diamond girls,' said Mum.
'Little sparkling gems, the lot of you . . .'

Dixie, Rochelle, Jude and Martine – the
Diamond girls! They might sound like a girl band
but these sisters' lives are anything but glamorous.
They've moved into a terrible house on a run-down
estate and after barely five minutes Rochelle's
flirting, Jude's fighting and Martine's storming off.
Even though Dixie's the youngest, she's desperate
to get the house fixed up before Mum comes home
with her new baby. Will the Diamond girls pull
together in time for the first Diamond boy?

'A compelling mix of gritty realism and warmth
where the chaos is largely redeemed by love'
Independent

'Wilson writes with such humour and affection
for her characters that this book is full of
unexpected joy' *Daily Mail*

ISBN 978 0 552 55376 6

JACKY DAYDREAM

Jacqueline Wilson

Illustrated by Nick Sharratt

Everybody knows Tracy Beaker, Jacqueline Wilson's best-loved character. But what do they know about Jacqueline herself? In this fascinating book, discover . . .

. . . how Jacky played with paper dolls like **April** in *Dustbin Baby*.

. . . how she dealt with an unpredictable father like **Prue** in *Love Lessons*.

. . . how she sat entrance exams like **Ruby** in *Double Act*.

But most of all how **Jacky** loved reading and writing stories. Losing herself in a new world was the best possible way she could think of spending her time. From the very first story she wrote, *Meet the Maggots*, it was clear that this little girl had a very vivid imagination. But who would've guessed that she would grow up to be the mega-bestselling, award-winning JacquelineWilson!

AVAILABLE FROM DOUBLEDAY BOOKS
978 0 385 61015 5

WIN

ONE OF 50 SIGNED COPIES OF
TOTALLY JACQUELINE WILSON

Totally Jacqueline Wilson is the brand-new book that every Jacqueline Wilson fan will want to own. Published in November 2007, it features loads of great Jacky facts, fantastic new stories, activities and top tips, including a guide to how to draw like Nick Sharratt and how to create your own Jacqueline Wilson party!

To enter the competition, simply visit **www.jacquelinewilson.co.uk** and follow the online instructions.

Closing date: 28th September 2007

PLUS Check out the FREE online Jacqueline Wilson fan club at **www.jacquelinewilson.co.uk**
With an interactive diary, message board and all the latest news on Jacqueline Wilson, it's the coolest place to make new friends, share gossip and talk to other Jacqueline Wilson fans.